WAR-LORDS

SIMA QIAN

War-Lords

TRANSLATED

WITH TWELVE OTHER STORIES

FROM HIS HISTORICAL RECORDS

BY WILLIAM DOLBY

AND JOHN SCOTT

EDINBURGH

Southside

1974

SOUTHSIDE (PUBLISHERS) LTD
2 Lamb's Pend, Penicuik, Midlothian EH26 8HR
Scotland

First published Edinburgh 1974

I.S.B.N. 900025 08 5

Copyright © 1974: Historical Introduction A. W. E. Dolby; Literary and Critical Introduction J. H. J. Scott; All other Contents A. W. E. Dolby and J. H. J. Scott.

Printed in Great Britain by T. & A. Constable Ltd, Hopetoun Street, Edinburgh EH7 4NF

DEDICATED
BY TRANSLATORS & PUBLISHERS TO

HERMANN PÁLSSON

*vitmaðr mikill ok hógværr
ok hófsmaðr um alla hluti*

ACKNOWLEDGMENTS

Acknowledgments are due to the Clarendon Press, Oxford, for permission to quote from *Chan-kuo Ts'e*, tr. J. I. Crump jr, © 1970 Oxford University Press. In the passage quoted, all proper names have been romanised according to the same system as we have used throughout this book.   J.H.J.S.

Table of Contents

Historical Introduction	9
Literary and Critical Introduction	36

STRATEGISTS

Sun the Martial	55
Sun the Cripple	57
Wu Qi	60

WAR-LORDS

Lord Mengchang	69
Lord Flat Plain	87
Prince Fearless (Lord Trust Tumulus)	102
Lord Chunshen	115

ASSASSINS

Cao Mo	131
Zhuan Zhu	132
Yu Rang	134
Nie Zheng	137
Jing Ke	142

JESTERS

Baldy Chunyu	159
Jester Meng	162
Jester Twisty Pole	166

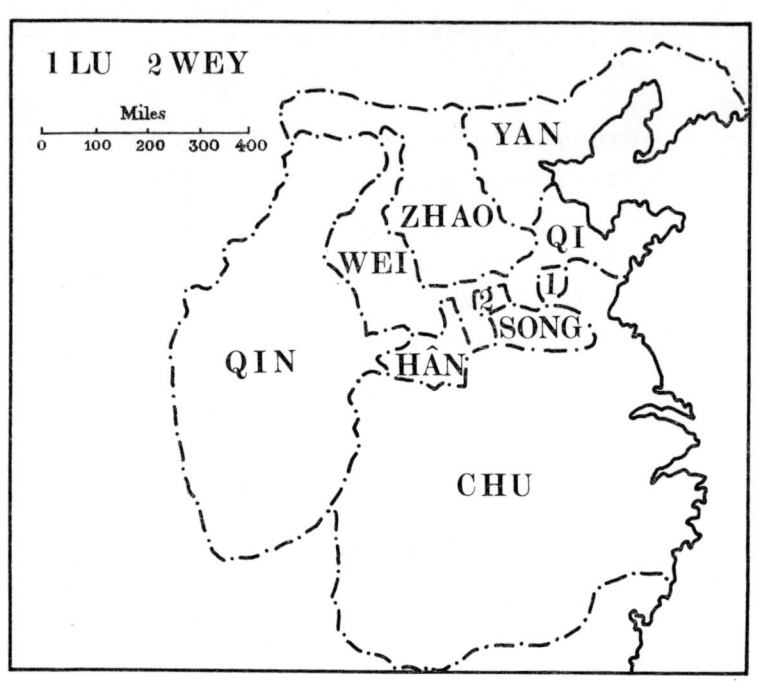

THE WARRING STATES

Historical Introduction

Power-mongering, fence-sitting war-lords, policy-peddling political clients, panacea-vendors, needle-fine Machiavellian intriguers, itinerant Nestors, down-at-heel wizards of statecraft, indeflectible assassins, ruthless pimps of *Realpolitik*, generals and tacticians of superb genius and cunning – dog-butchers, gamblers, tipplers, farmyard impersonators, medics, cat-burglars, jesters, masters of wisecrack, lascivious princesses, seductive concubines, philosophers, giants of the mind, immortals of the tongue, saints of astounding virtue and fortitude, and rogues of limitless treachery – all this is only a part of the cavalcade which we witness in the pages of Sima Qian's *Historical Records*, the ancient Chinese work from which we have taken the present selection of stories. Unchallengeably the father of Chinese historiography, Sima Qian was no mere tabulator of soulless statistics, no mere scavenger of faceless trends and movements. Instead he emphasised the realities and human drama of history. This he did with such mastery and skill and with such undying effect on later writing and story-telling that he is also undoubtedly one of the greatest fathers of many-sired Chinese literature. These present translations aim to stress his attractions as a teller of a good story, but since in our view, and clearly in his, a good story is often the best way to express the essence of historical truth, we are also putting his historical methods and ability on display.

Born in 147 B.C. and living till around 90 B.C., Sima Qian came into the world at Longmen, now Hancheng county in Shensi province, in the north of China, where his family farmed on the southern side of hills some way north of the Yellow River. He probably attended a village school there, but in 140 his father Sima Tan was appointed Grand Historian to the imperial court and moved his family to Xianwu village in Mouling, a suburb of Changan. Changan was in those days the capital of the Former Han dynasty, which ruled China from 206 B.C. until A.D. 8. There Sima Qian continued his education, and by the time he was nine he was able to read the most ancient writings in the awkward old scripts. No mean achievement.

From youth onwards he travelled very widely. When nineteen he visited the regions of present-day Kiangsu, Chekiang, Honan, and Shantung provinces, making extensive trips to historical and archaeological sites. In Shantung, besides taking part in an archery tournament, he came to close grips with the living traditions of Confucianism, China's major ideology throughout most of ancient history and on into modern times. This was the area where Confucius and his greatest successor Mencius had both been active, and experience of these traditions reinforced Sima Qian's literary and academic understanding of their profound philosophies. In this part of China he seems also to have run into some nasty trouble with brigands or thugs, which in its way provided him with additional food for historical thought, as seen at the end of the story of Lord Mengchang and elsewhere. His return route was through modern Honan and Hupeh provinces.

Either by taking examinations or through his father's influence he obtained a "cadet" appointment as Imperial Secretary in government service and in 111 B.C. accompanied a military expedition to the area of present Szechwan and Yunan provinces. These were the home of many non-Chinese and anti-Chinese people, and were viewed by northern Chinese as dangerous, alien climes, almost the other end of the earth. Career and his own avid curiosity thus took him the length and breadth of China on journeys which were invaluable for confirming his historical knowledge and acumen and for stimulating his interest. Considering the poor communications and political and racial diversity of those times the extent of his travels is quite remarkable. First-hand acquaintance with local tradition and archaeological remains was an important part of his historiographical thoroughness.

In the spring of 110 B.C. a momentous event took place. For the first time in the history of the Han Dynasty, the Martial Emperor, Wu-di [140 – 87], held the Great Dynastic Sacrifice to Heaven at sacred Mount Tai in Shantung. This was a symbolic declaration that the dynasty was Heaven-created and Heaven-approved, and it meant a great deal for his prestige. Wu-di had previously consulted his learned courtiers and scholars on what form the sacrificial ceremonies should

HISTORICAL INTRODUCTION

take, but had in the end rejected their suggestions and devised his own ritual. Probably Sima Tan was one of the leading advisers whose ideas the Emperor brushed aside. Whether because of some such disagreement, or because of some physical disability, he was unable to attend the Great Sacrifice, and missing it upset him so much that he fell mortally ill.

His son, however, took part in the sacrifice. After delivering a report on the military expedition at the capital, Sima Qian went eastwards to Mount Tai. On his way he called on his father, who was staying at Loyang. Tan clasped his hand and in tears urged that when he himself was dead Qian should continue his life-project. This was the writing of a history of the past few hundred years in succession to the various works of historical import attributed to Confucius. Tan had clearly done a great deal of preparatory work on this magnificent enterprise, collecting numerous chronicles of the old Zhou Dynasty [1027 – 256 B.C.] and other material. Qian swore to do as enjoined. That was the last time he met his father, as Tan died in the summer or autumn of 110 B.C.

In 108, after the three-year mourning period, Sima Qian succeeded his father as Grand Historian. What sort of a job was it? In an extant letter written in 93 B.C., a most moving piece of writing, he complains:

My father never did any great deeds to earn himself a tally of lofty authority or to get his name written in the lists of hereditary privilege. And being a scribe and annalist concerned with astronomy and the calendar, one is little removed from the diviners and priests, bound to be the object of the monarch's sport and play, kept like any entertainer or court jester and despised by the vulgar. If I had been executed, it would have been like nine oxen losing a single hair. I was no different from a mole-cricket or an ant.

Yet from other indications it was clearly a position of considerable importance, for all that its importance may not have afforded him any general esteem or protection. The prime duties seem to have been those of astronomy and calendrical calculations, with the keeping of historical records, if anything, a secondary activity. At dawn on 25 December 105 a new calendar was formally established. In a basically agricultural society beset by the constant threat of massive natural disasters, the ability to predict natural phenomena and order seasonal activities contributed greatly to a ruler's prestige. Astronomy, astrology, and likewise the calendar had a mystic and psychological importance of a magnitude which it is difficult for a modern person to grasp. Sima Qian was the main creator of the new calendar of 105. It has been used in China since then with scarcely a break, until, in modern times, it was challenged by the Gregorian Calendar.

Once this was out of the way, the writing of the History became his main preoccupation and ambition. He now had full and immediate access to the Imperial libraries and archives. For the next few years he devoted himself to the History, but in 99 B.C. he suffered a devastating blow. In that year the Xiongnu or Huns, constant enemies of the Han Empire along its northern and north-western frontiers, were giving considerable trouble and had inflicted one great defeat on the Chinese. The Chinese general Li Ling was sent, in command of a small force of only a few thousand men, to combat the Hunnish hordes. He marched deep into enemy territory, performing prodigious military feats and inflicting heavy losses. There were joyful celebrations when news of this reached the Han court, but soon Li Ling's supplies ran out, and, in the absence of any relieving forces, he succumbed to the enemy. Only four hundred of his men managed to return, while he himself, aware of the fate that awaited defeated generals under the Martial Emperor, surrendered to the Xiongnu. The Martial Emperor was sick with fury. Sima Qian was an erstwhile colleague and acquaintance though by no means a close friend of Li Ling's. In a sublimely noble but ill-timed gesture he spoke up alone for the much-maligned general.

Not only was his defence of Li Ling entirely unwelcome; his words were also taken as implied criticism of another general, Li Guangli, for having failed to provide the reinforcements which could have averted Li Ling's defeat. Since this general was a brother of the Emperor's favourite concubine, the misunderstanding (if such it was) was doubly

HISTORICAL INTRODUCTION

unfortunate. The Emperor had Sima Qian thrown into jail for the crime of "deceiving the monarch", punishable by death.

In jail the historian experienced all the degradations of the helpless prisoner at the mercy of his jailers. In those times it was often possible for the rich to buy commutation of sentence, but he lacked the money, and none of his friends or acquaintances came forward to help him. Lamentably, but not altogether surprisingly, none of those who had access to the Emperor did so much as put in a good word for him. Somehow, though, he avoided the death penalty. Perhaps the Emperor felt that he and his vast knowledge were too valuable to throw to the executioner or, quite probably, Sima Qian himself requested the substitution of another punishment, one scarcely less vile. The sentence was changed to castration. It was carried out in a place euphemistically referred to as the "silkworm chamber".

Life for the eunuch was in many ways worse than death. Quite apart from the lasting, deleterious physical effects, the general scorn and shame associated with the punishment and with his condition were a terrible burden for anyone with the slightest sensitivity to bear and Sima Qian was beyond doubt very sensitive and fine of thought. This raises a very curious problem. For someone so fine and so sensitive as Sima Qian death would surely have seemed preferable to living death as a disgraced *castrato?* Suicide would have been a quite normal, honourable, and acceptable way out. He himself remarks in his letter:

Although I may be feeble and cowardly, trying to hang on to life like this, I know very well what a man ought to do and what he ought to avoid doing. So how was it that I allowed myself to sink into iniquity and the shame of fetters? And since even a slave-woman, a drudge, or a kitchen-maid can put an end to her own life, it would certainly not be beyond someone like me. The reason why I stuck it out and lingered on in this living death, letting myself live on in the shit and muck of it all, was that I loathed the idea of departing with thoughts, desires, and feelings in my heart still not given their full expression, and because I despised the notion of quitting the world without displaying my literary master-work for posterity....

In my immodest unworthiness, I reposed so much confidence in my own ineffective powers of literary expression that, having snared and netted together all the world's old and neglected stories, I examined them in the light of currently accepted facts, investigated the reasons for the rise and fall of political power, and the vicissitudinous historical patterns which they embodied, and shaped the whole collection into one hundred and thirty chapters in all. In doing so it was my desire to go thoroughly into universal natural and human relationships, to reach a deep understanding of the great crises and decisive upheavals of ancient and modern times, and to formulate all these things into one whole work according to one consistent philosophical approach. The initial draft was not yet completed when I met with this catastrophe. I was reluctant to leave it unfinished, and that is why I delivered myself up to that extreme punishment with no expression of bitter resentment on my face.

When I have finally completed the writing of this work, I shall deposit it in the Famous Mountains, and, should it become widely known through the thriving regions and great cities of the people there, then would I have been compensated for the shame of the punishment which I have lately suffered, and were I to undergo ten thousand more mutilations I should still feel no regret whatsoever. But these are things which one can convey only to men of insight and understanding. No good trying to explain them to ordinary people!

"Famous Mountains" is a puzzle. It may mean the famous sacred peaks of ancient China or some particular one of them. Perhaps he intended for safety of preservation to distribute his work all over the country or to place it on out-of-the-way spots where it would be less liable to the destructive effects of political changes. Alternatively it may simply be a name for an imperial library. In any case, Sima Qian's letter makes it quite clear that the completion of his history was probably his only reason for wanting to carry on living.

Perhaps even the violent and autocratic Martial Emperor repented of what he had done to the historian. After his castration, Sima Qian was appointed Head of the Palace Central Secretariat, a position in which he

HISTORICAL INTRODUCTION

enjoyed great honour and favours from the Emperor and was entrusted with considerable responsibilities. All the same, the remainder of his life must have been a wretched twilight, as another passage from the letter describes:

And, you know, it is not easy to put up with the existence of one who has tumbled to the depths, for the mean and vile are full of nasty slanders and gossip about one. By the words which I spoke I brought this tragedy upon myself, and now into the bargain I bring shame on my father's name by letting myself be cut to pieces with mockery from my own villagers. How can I have the face to approach my father's and mother's tombs ever again? Let a hundred ages go by, and the filth and defilement of it all will still be all-pervading. The thought of such things wrenches my guts round nine times a day: when I sit at home, it leaves me blurred and dazed, and whenever I go out, it robs me of any sense of purpose or direction.

Every time I reflect on this humiliation, the sweat never fails to pour down my back and soak my coat. I would prefer it if I could take myself away and hide deep in some mountain cave, rather than be as I am, only fit to be a harem eunuch. But instead I make do and bob up and down with the vulgar stream and bow this way and that in conformity with the fashion of the moment, so as to keep in step with their madness and delusions. You, Shao Qing, bid me try to push fine men into positions of importance, but might that not rather do harm to my own private aim? Even if I now tried to cover up for myself with fancy talk and high-flown phrases and endeavoured to explain away my condition with pretty excuses, it would be no use. Ordinary people wouldn't believe them, and I would merely be inviting more humiliation. In short, the rights and wrongs of my case will only be given their just settlement when I am dead and gone. Writing is an inadequate means of expressing all that I would like to say, but I venture to present you with some slight picture of my paltry views on these matters.

Sima Qian completed his great enterprise before he died. One daughter was his only child, as far as we know. After his death the *Historical Records* gradually became known to the public. Some time during the period 73 – 54 B.C. his daughter's son, Yang Yun, Marquis of Pingtong, promoted it, and it acquired wide circulation. The usurper Wang Mang, who toppled the Han Dynasty for a brief interregnum (A.D. 9 – 23), sought out Sima Qian's main surviving descendant and honoured him with the title Viscount Master of History. The greatest amends made to Sima Qian, however, were the praise and reverence lavished by posterity on his masterpiece.

Something of the magnitude and ambition of Sima Qian's endeavour can be understood if we realise that it was intended as a history of the whole past of the whole world. The qualifications to this statement scarcely reduce its impact. Of course it was the whole known world. But for a Chinese of those times China was more or less the world. There lay the greatest mass of population, and there shone the most elaborate and refined culture known. Other peripheral peoples no doubt seemed to be almost incidental to China, though Sima Qian was certainly aware of their distinctive qualities and virtues. He does not mention the great Greek or Roman empires or Japan. Either he knew nothing of them or knew of them only by strange or dubious legends, which his historiographical integrity rejected as unworthy of inclusion. In any case, the influence from these other civilisations was certainly inadequate to upset the view that China was the main centre of the world, all the world that mattered for that world. This need not surprise us or inspire our indignation. Sima Qian's limitation was not that of gross prejudice, simply one of the unavailability of knowledge. And a vast scope was left him, all the same.

Apart from a few sections on non-Chinese peoples his history concentrates on China. He attempts to go as far back as he feels he reasonably can in what he considered fairly secure or explicit knowledge and legend. He does not go into the ultimates of creation and the origins of mankind, but we need not presume that he had never thought about such things or had no ideas on them. There were certainly theories in contemporary circulation. Caution and humility no doubt led him to exclude such considerations as not within the scope of his work. On the other hand, in reaching back into the blur of the distant past, he does use material which strikes one as distinctly mythical. He begins with the period of the Five Emperors [traditionally from 2852 to 2208 B.C.], then proceeds to deal with the Xia Dynasty [traditionally from 2205 to 1766 B.C.], the Shang Dynasty [traditionally from 1766 to 1028 B.C.], the Zhou Dynasty [traditionally from 1027 to 256 B.C.], the Qin Dynasty [221 – 207 B.C.], and finally with the Han Dynasty up to his own times. The last three dynasties are fully attested by other literary works. His accounts of the Five Emperors and Xia Dynasty contain much that is clearly legendary and he treats it often with so much obvious caution that he cannot entirely have trusted it.

Before we deride his credulity, or blame him for having included any such material in a history, perhaps it would be well to recall that the legends which he incorporates are not necessarily of no historical value. The written evidence of the Shang Dynasty was gravely doubted by some scholars until archaeological discoveries in the late nineteenth century provided irrefutable confirmation of much of it. If the Xia existed, it was quite probably pre-literate or barely literate, and the hope of archaeological corroboration is small. None the less, the written legends may well reflect the story of some part or tributary stream of China's past, however disguised or altered by supernatural and other overlaying. Similarly in the case of the Five Emperors. True, it is now agreed that these rulers were originally local deities later semi-humanised, but there again local deities are often deifications of human ancestors. Careful modern history shows again and again that seeming myth is often a close reflection of reality, and valuable source material, if only one can disentangle it and interpret it in the right way. Perhaps some such feeling was at least part of Sima Qian's motivation. He includes the legends, some of them, and suppresses their more grossly superstitious elements. Another value of their inclusion for historians, of course, is that superstitious legend can have very tangible real effects on later attitudes, and on the course of subsequent history.

It was a formidable task to put such a vast period of time with its broad range of complex considerations into one coherent work. To surmount the difficulty Sima Qian organised the material in an ingenious and in many ways highly effective manner. The one hundred and thirty chapters of the *Historical Records* are divided up into five sections. The first, containing twelve chapters, is the Basic Annals. These are the chronicles and barer bones of the political history of the houses that ruled China during the various periods. Included also is an account of the Hegemon King Xiang Yu, who although never an emperor, did hold actual power over China for a brief period at the end of the Qin Dynasty. The Basic Annals provide the broad outline and the other four sections serve to fill in and elaborate the picture.

Next come ten chapters of Chronological Tables, providing parallel lists under date-headings of political events in the various feudal states of the Zhou Dynasty, and lists under fief-headings of nobles who held fiefs during the Han Dynasty, the nobles being listed in chronological order. At the head of some of these tables are brief essays which give a deep insight into Sima Qian's historiographical principles. Third come eight chapters of Monographs on technical subjects, such as rites, music, the calendar and canals, sacrifices, economics, and so on.

A further thirty chapters make up the Hereditary Houses section. During the latter half of the Zhou Dynasty actual political power had passed from the hands of the Zhou imperial rulers to the rulers of the feudal states which made up China. This section gives chronicles of the ruling houses of these individual states in the same way as the Basic Annals gives them for the rulers of all China as a whole. Two seeming odd-men-out are also in this section: Confucius and a Qin Dynasty rebel named Chen She. Confucius was the spiritual founder of the orthodox philosophy of the Han Dynasty, and Chen She was in a sense the military and political ancestor of that dynasty. Both had been major forces in the attempt to destroy the preceding Qin Dynasty – Confucius by the opposition of his philosophical heirs to the brutal Legalist philosophy of the Qin. Both seem to have been included because their heritage, like that of the feudal houses, was of long duration.

HISTORICAL INTRODUCTION

The final, largest, and in many ways finest section of the *Historical Records* is the Memoirs or *Vitae*, consisting of seventy chapters. If the rest of the history is mainly concerned with general theory and political facts and figures, this section provides the complementary human and literary synthesis. Some of the chapters are on foreign kingdoms, one is an autobiography of Sima Qian himself, and one is on finance, but by and large they are concerned with the great deeds, sayings, and dramas of individuals and their effect on historical situations. Sometimes the individuals are lumped together under generic headings, such as "assassins", "jesters", "harsh officials", "Confucian disciples". It was into the Memoirs that the historian put most of his heart. His particular stress is on the contribution of the individual to historical change. This does not make him a Victorian worshipper of "great men". He is not so concerned with mundane greatness of rank, title, and status, but rather with greatness of wit and character. As often as not he makes social nonentities his heroes. For him drop-outs and peasants, dog-butchers, and burglars may just as well be the catalysts or guiding hands of history as kings, ministers, and generals.

The Memoirs are in many ways the climax of the whole history, for they embody most clearly, in striking human terms, the philosophical aims that were Sima Qian's major purpose in writing the history. Sima Qian is unashamedly didactic, and his own opinions are made very clear not only through his selection and use of material and by occasional comments within the stories but also by carefully isolated passages at the end of them, prefaced with the words "Here follows the Grand Historian's commentary", which contain his own and other's own views on the moral import and other meanings of the tales.

The extent of Sima Qian's didactic ambitions and the lofty light in which he viewed his history can be appreciated when one realises that he quite openly proclaimed himself the successor of Confucius, then the greatest literary and moral figure of China's entire past. This would seem deplorably immodest, if he had not been so nobly determined and uniquely situated to substantiate the claim. At the end of his chapter on the life of Confucius he remarks:

In the Book of Odes it says, 'When you see a high mountain, you can raise your eyes towards it. When you see an open road, you can make out your direction along it.' Yes, even if you know you cannot ever quite get there, your heart knows it is the right direction to aim for. When I read the works of Confucius, I used to long to get to know him as a person. On visiting Lu, seeing his temple, chariots, robes, and ritual vessels, and witnessing all the students studying the rites and proprieties in his home, I could not drag myself away and lingered on, unable to depart. There have been a mass of emperors, monarchs, and great men in the world who in their day enjoyed splendour and glory and once dead were forgotten. The influence of Confucius, for all that he was a commoner and wore no fancy robes of high office, has endured, and for more than ten generations scholars have taken him as their master and source of inspiration. Anyone in China, be he king, prince, or lord, who discusses the ancient classics, takes Confucius as the final authority. No doubt about his deserving the title 'Supreme Sage'.

Sima Qian identified himself with Confucius not only spiritually but also in the course both their lives took. "He who exposes others' faults, puts himself in danger," he says of Confucius – a close parallel to the nature of his own personal tragedy. Elsewhere he explicitly and elaborately identifies many of his own historiographical objectives with those attributed to Confucius. In his chapter of autobiography he quotes, with allusion to himself, the following passage, which he attributes to the philosopher Dong Zongshu [176 – 104 B.C.]:

Confucius was chief Judicial Officer in Lu at the time when the political fibre and fortunes of the house of Zhou lay in decay and ruins, and the rulers of the various states only regarded him as a pest and their great ministers only obstructed him with awkwardnesses. Realising that his specific suggestions were not going to be adopted and that his overall theories and policies were not going to be put into effect, he made critical and moral assessments of two hundred and forty years of the past as a way of setting up a standard for the world. In these he condemned emperors, pulled feudal monarchs down a peg, and castigated great ministers with the sole purpose

HISTORICAL INTRODUCTION

of fully proclaiming the right and proper way to govern. 'Rather than express it in abstract theoretical terms,' he himself once said, 'I prefer to demonstrate it through the depth, immediacy, and obvious clarity of actual historical events.'

The parallel with Sima Qian, especially in the last lines, is a strong one. What ideology lies, then, behind Sima Qian's history? Is it Confucianism? The problem has been and is the subject of fierce controversy. In his autobiography he quotes at great length his father's analysis of the main schools of philosophy, and this gives a heavy preponderance to Taoism. As a filial son, and since he chooses to quote this analysis, Sima Qian might be regarded as a Taoist. His next great successor as a historian in fact bluntly accuses him of being such. The question is happily a somewhat futile one. Sima Qian's father's assessment of the philosophies in fact sees good points in all of them. Clearly so did the son. He was not one to put carts before horses or dogma before the whole purpose of having a philosophy at all. Like so many Chinese he was delightfully eclectic, choosing from wherever he could whatever pleased him. If he sometimes seems Confucian and sometimes Taoist, it is because these philosophies, too, were not watertight compartments, but shared some common, broadly human aims. Some of the fundamental concepts of worldly Confucianism are remarkably similar to those of non-worldly Taoism, partly because both seek to relate the human condition to similar notions of the universal order, and partly because both seem motivated by a similar warm sympathy for humanity.

War and violence are often the setting for these stories, but they are not their lesson. The violence serves rather as a foil for other, more admirable human qualities. Sima Qian persistently champions apparent underdogs, those who show kindness, and those who in crushing circumstances maintain their integrity. He himself comes through as a humorous, humane man who revels in individual ingenuity and loves any good story. These are the characteristics which, with his literary genius and scholarly caution, have made him one of China's best-loved writers and given him such a powerful influence on later writing.

The spirit of Sima Qian's work has been a constant inspiration to Chinese historians, and its formal organisation, aims, and methods have in many ways moulded the whole of official Chinese historical writing. That China's magnificent tradition of official history-writing arose and survived at all is very likely due to his example.

Once the *Historical Records* became popular there were many attempts at emulating them. The earliest one of note is that of Ban Gu [A.D. 32 – 92], who took up where his father Ban Biao had left off, and wrote a *History of the Former Han*. This not only used large chunks from the *Historical Records* but modelled much of its form on it. All the basic divisions were retained, except the Hereditary Houses. But Ban Gu confined himself to one dynasty only. His was the first of the dynastic histories. In subsequent ages it became the custom for each major dynasty to produce an officially-sponsored history of the dynasty preceding it. The scope was that of Ban Gu, but Sima Qian remained a great source of inspiration. A single dynasty was more manageable and more within the range of the general run of historians, though in later ages official historians had the assistance of a considerable staff. Few could have matched Sima Qian's sweeping vision and control. It was not until the historian Sima Guang (A.D. 1019 – 86] wrote his *Comprehensive Mirror for the Aid of Government* that another major overall history was written. Completed in 1085, it gave a panorama of China's past from 403 B.C. to A.D. 959. Zheng Qiao [A.D. 1108 – 66] also wrote a *Comprehensive Annals*, a monumental history in the manner of the *Historical Records*.

Later dynastic histories were trammelled by the somewhat artificial limitation to one dynasty. The later monumental histories do not quite match the sparkle and freshness of Sima Qian. Most later histories were written by men under the influence of the somewhat austere Neo-Confucian orthodoxy, or were men who tended to notice the mighty of rank a little too much and the mighty of soul a little too little. They are a treasury of magnificent writings, but in some respects they pale as whole works besides the *Historical Records*. Sima Qian bitterly attacks many of the policies and methods of his Emperor. Later emperors were

HISTORICAL INTRODUCTION

consequently very wary of their historians, and this had a decidedly restrictive effect on the historians' freedom of expression.

Such factors tended to limit Sima Qian's influence on formal history, and it was the popular, looser, less serious histories that were sometimes able to follow him more freely. Perhaps formal history is an unreal compartment? Perhaps only what we call literature is a vague enough category to embrace the whole of human complexity? Sima Qian often presents history in the form of exquisitely constructed, drama-packed tales, their narrative quality reinforced by profound characterisation, humour, tragedy, and an ingenious interlinking with other stories in a saga-like fashion that gives enormous depth of association to a comparatively small amount of words. These are achievements perhaps more easily emulated by the story-teller and playwright than by the official historian. Scholars throughout the ages and especially in modern times have cast doubts on the historicity of much of the *Historical Records* (a title given the work after Sima Qian had died). The detail of some of the Memoirs is particularly called in doubt. For all the care and scepticism with which Sima Qian undoubtedly approached many of his sources, there is a strong case for supposing that he sometimes embroidered fairly freely and that he sometimes used popular stories and other dubious material with no known reliable corroboration and even in conflict with more solidly known historical facts. He may well have created some of his stories from entirely or largely fictitious popular tales and saga cycles. At least one scholar suggests that Sima Qian used the exercises of professional sophists, which may have had very little connexion with historical realities.[1] Of course the popular tales and so on may well have contained or reflected solid historical fact: but often one is tempted to regard Sima Qian rather as a brilliant writer of fiction than as an historian. Certainly the debt owed by fiction and drama to his work in later ages reflect its affinities with them. The great critic Jin Shengtan described the *Historical Records* in 1640 as one

---

[1] See Crump, J. I. *Intrigues: Studies of the Chan-kuo Ts'e*, Michigan 1964.

of the "six great books of literary genius", along with the poem of the *Li-sao*, the work of Taoist philosophy and scintillating anecdote known as the *Zhuang-zi*, the poems of Du Fu, the bawdy play *West Wing*, and the rumbustious, picaresque novel *Water Margin*.

Features traceable to Sima Qian's influence are found in much of early fiction, but the saga characteristics of his work made it more akin in spirit to the novel than to the short story. Doubtless the market story-tellers of the Song Dynasty [A.D. 960 – 1279], some of whom specialised in historical tales, drew heavily upon him. Among the earliest examples of long prose fiction in China are the *ping-hua* books printed in the early fourteenth century, with titles such as *Seven States and Spring and Autumn*, *Qin Annexes the Six States*, and *History of the Former Han*. Although these are often very loosely plotted and crudely constructed, and although they sometimes use the very colloquial language of their era, they reveal a great debt to ancient official historians, particularly Sima Qian, not only in the general *traits* of their stories but frequently by their use of whole unaltered chunks from an ancient history. One, after a few lines of verse, starts off with the words "The Historian Academician Sima Qian said . . .". Scholars hotly debate whether these stories were actually the stuff of market story-tellers, their prompt books, or chap-books. There is no doubt of their importance in the birth of the colloquial novel, which appeared first around the middle of the fourteenth century. The first novels written solely as literary works derived some of their material and possibly the whole idea of their conception from the *ping-hua*.

With their tight dramatic structure, their masterly control of tension and their exciting climaxes, many of Sima Qian's stories could easily be adapted into stage plays, and his influence on the development of Chinese drama was, if anything, greater than on that of the novel. The titles of some proto-dramas which are no longer extant indicate the possibility of such influence; and when the first mature form of drama arose in China during the thirteenth century a good number of plays were based on his stories, some of them, such as *Yu Rang Swallows Charcoal*, by Yang Zi, and the anonymous *Horse Mound Road*, on tales translated in the present collection. The final climax of *Yu Rang Swallows Charcoal* sometimes very closely paraphrases Sima Qian and shows other strong traces of borrowing from him. In subsequent centuries drama continued to renew its indebtedness to him. A play called *Cold are the Waters of Change* by Ye Xianzu [A.D. 1566 – 1641] follows our story of Jing Ke, often using the words of Sima Qian unaltered, but contriving by means of supernatural elements to provide a happy ending. Few forms of Chinese literature did not derive something from him. The popularity of his stories nowadays in the annotated collections of classical Chinese prose suggests that he will continue to have a living effect on creative writing.

The stories which we have translated all come from the Memoirs section of the *Historical Records* and all are about the latter part of the Zhou Dynasty. Sima Qian's history mainly concerns two contrasting periods: the troubled, divided China of the late Zhou, and the united empire of the early Han Dynasty. Sima Qian lived in an age that was the opposite extreme to the chaos and internecine strife of the late Zhou. Under the Martial Emperor, China was a vigorous, expanding, outward-looking empire. Its frontiers were rapidly extending into Korea and deep into Central Asia, and its defences were being stiffened. Campaigns were mounted against the Xiongnu, and there prevailed a bold curiosity about foreign parts which led to some wide-ranging exploratory expeditions as far as the Caspian Sea. Within the country strong measures were taken to reinforce central government, while the prestige and splendour of the State was enhanced by momentous sacrifices and ceremonial pomp, and by the building of fine palaces, mansions, and parks. As a step towards an official State ideology, the Emperor gave Confucianism his patronage; and he also made tours across China proclaiming and consolidating imperial power and glory.

As with many countries at the zenith of their political power, the glory was to some extent a *façade* on grimmer realities. Military successes were one side, the cost in life and taxes the other. Pomp and circumstance and the glorification of worldly institutions were fertile soil for hypocrisy, servility, and sterile hierarchies. Sima Qian seems to have looked with some nostalgia back to the Zhou dynasty, when the very fluidity of political conditions and the desperate lack of peace, social solidity, and entrenched moral codes placed people under the kind of pressures and provided them with the kind of opportunities which seem to have tempered the character and refined the mind to an extraordinary degree. In spite of all the warfare, the late Zhou was China's classical age, the period when her fundamental philosophies and some of her greatest literary works appeared and she laid the main foundations of her thought and culture. The testing times produced much spiritual greatness and gigantic individuality, in contrast to the half-and-half moralities that Sima Qian saw so often in more settled, unified China.

He was a fierce critic of his own age. Some have seen this as a reflection of his bitterness towards the Martial Emperor for the savage treatment which he personally received. No doubt his personal tragedy distilled and intensified his judgments, but he seems to have written much of his history before he was sentenced. Most of his indignation and many of his enthusiasms by no means lacked firm rational foundations. He admired the rugged, free spirit of the late Zhou and despised its opposite in the Han. True, he has an unusual sympathy for underdogs and down-and-outs, cripples, dwarfs, music-mongers, and all those who, like himself, have suffered misfortune and injustice, but suffering often renders the character more varied, humane, and otherwise admirable. He points out that most of the great literary figures of the past were inspired by their sorrows and sufferings. The parallel with himself is obvious, but his sympathies, in this respect, have some universal reference.

The Zhou Dynasty also began as a powerful empire. Its rulers originated from present Shensi province and were originally feudatories of the Shang Dynasty. Eventually they become strong enough to challenge the Shang. Over a period of ten years they first conquered the various allies of the Shang, and then in 1122 B.C. defeated the Shang king, driving him to suicide. The early Zhou rulers and the statesman Duke of Zhou provided a period of energetic government, but fourteen years or so after the foundation of the Dynasty the King gave numerous territorial fiefs to his kinsmen and firmly established the feudal system. There was a long stable reign from 1001 to 947 B.C., but a few decades later the fortunes of the central government were in clear decline. In 842 a popular rebellion forced the King to flee his capital. In 771 another King was assassinated, and the following year his successor transferred the capital to Luoyi in the present Henan province. This date, 770, serves to mark the end of the Zhou Kings' real military and political power. For the rest of the Dynasty they ruled only a very small territory, and as little more than mere figureheads of the nation as a whole. From 770 onwards the various feudal lords held actual power, and divided up the country between them.

The remainder of the Dynasty is often referred to as the Eastern Zhou, in distinction to the earlier period called the Western Zhou. Historians divide the Eastern Zhou into two periods; the Spring and Autumn Period [770 – 481 B.C.] and the Warring States Period [480 – 222 B.C.]. There were no less than one hundred and forty-seven feudal states, some of very minor proportions, but most of these were early on absorbed, annexed, or dominated by the bigger and stronger ones. During the Spring and Autumn Period political struggles and warfare were on a fairly limited scale. Fighting was neither very efficient nor in general very extreme in its objectives and was governed by restrained and civilised codes of honour. Positions of power and command were still largely within the hands of hereditary nobility. One or other of the big States would often establish a hegemony over the others, though the totality of this hegemony has sometimes been exaggerated by later writers. A Duke of Qi, a Duke of Song, a Duke of Jin, a Duke of Qin, and a King of Chu, who reigned respectively from 684 to 682, from 650 to 637, from 636 to 628, from 659 to 621, and from 613 to 591 B.C., are commonly referred to as the Five Hegemons. The States of Wu and Yue also established limited hegemonies in the later years of the Spring and Autumn Period.

From around 470 the struggle condensed itself into a mammoth competition between seven powerful States, the Seven Cock-birds: Qin, Chu, Yan, Qi, Zhao, Wei, and Hân. The warfare intensified, techniques of weaponry and command advanced rapidly, and the scale of slaughter grew much heavier. Alliances were formed and broken again and again. Diplomats and itinerant politicians – the "persuaders" – roamed from court to court trying to persuade rulers to adopt their astute policies. Teachers of rhetoric, philosophers, generals, strategic experts, ambitious knights, and many others likewise trapesed from capital to capital offering their skills, wooing and wooed. In these more desperate and demanding times ability gained ground over heredity and social caste. Rulers realised that they needed men of ability, to enable their States to survive. The ability to attract and recognise military, diplomatic, and political ability became of paramount importance.

Power was not always in the hands of the rulers. War-lords with their vast retinues of well-chosen clients and advisers were often the key figures in the game. Courts overflowed with wealth and luxury, their denizens living riotously as if every day were their last, while huge parts of the population lived in desperate poverty and wretchedness. At the same time the area of China was rapidly expanding, technology was making great strides, most significantly in the use of iron, and civilisation was growing more and more complex, demanding more sophisticated techniques of administration. Amid this change and turmoil the State of Qin eventually mopped up all the other States one by one. In 256 the last Zhou King surrendered, and by 221 Qin had destroyed all rivals. The King of Qin proclaimed himself First Emperor, and for the first time in her history China was firmly unified under a strong central government.

In retrospect there seems something inevitable about the eventual triumph of the semi-barbarian State of Qin with its ideology of Draconian, totalitarian Legalism, its Nazi-like ruthlessness and military efficiency, its steady absorption of talent from other States, and its favourable geographical position in the rich, mountainous north-west. Yet when one looks closer, one feels at times that it could have gone any

HISTORICAL INTRODUCTION

way. Qin often lost battles, and if there was any inevitability about the final outcome, it lay more in the dilly-dallying, mutual distrust, internecine squabbling, lack of diplomatic cohesion, and often the sheer inertia of other States than in their lack of military power. Or so it may seem. The tantalising possibility that it might have gone other ways, coupled no doubt with the burning wish that it had done, was surely one of the main things that made the Warring States Period so fascinating to Sima Qian. It is a grand drama, a tragedy in the Racinian sense. All the audience knows the dreadful end from the very beginning, but hope dies hard, and one finds oneself constantly trying to will another consummation to the plot. Or is it a pure tragedy? Or does Sima Qian give that extra final twist to the plot so characteristic of Chinese dramas in which a final glimpse of light conquers blackest despair? Does Jester Twisty Pole have the last word?

Our selection of stories opens with three military experts. Western scholarship often refers to the Memoirs as "lives" or "biographies", but sometimes they contain no more than a few scintillating anecdotes characterising the person and his major achievements, or just telling a good yarn with the loan of his name. It was certainly not Sima Qian's intention to write detailed biographies, cluttered with circumstantial detail. What is he trying to pick out in the Strategists? Adherence to purpose, strategic ingenuity, the commander's psychological insight, the ability to preserve and further oneself in ruthless times, and the grim humour that seems part of flexible military genius. His comment at the end of the section tempts one to conclude that he had a strong fellow-feeling for Sun the Cripple, and perhaps felt that Wu Qi's downfall had lessons for such as the Martial Emperor.

Sun the Martial is a name that resounds through Chinese history. The *Thirteen Treatises on War* attributed to him have had an immense influence on Chinese military thinking. That arch tactical genius Cao Cao [A.D. 155 – 220] wrote a commentary on them. In modern times

Mao Tse-tung has praised them highly and derived considerable inspiration from them. Western military experts have also given them considerable attention. B. H. Lidell Hart, that prolific writer on methods and men of war, once advised a Chinese military *attaché* under Chiang Kai-shek to read this classic. He considered that it embodied almost as much about the fundamentals of strategy and tactics as he himself had covered in more than twenty books and remarked that the *Thirteen Treatises* were "the best short introduction to the study of warfare, and no less valuable for constant reference in extending study of the subject". An American general has translated the *Thirteen Treatises* with various of the Chinese commentaries.[1] There is some doubt as to whether Sun the Martial was actually its author. Some suggest it may have been Sun the Cripple, but it is certainly 4th century B.C. or earlier.

The core of our translations is a section devoted to four War-Lords. All were contemporaneous, all were active in the life-and-death struggles towards the very last days of the Zhou Dynasty, and all competed with each other in building up private armies of political and military clients. All at times made more noise than the monarchs of their respective countries. They play chess with the balance of power. They move sometimes with lofty loyalties, at other times in sheer opportunism. They might easily have created states of their own, or paved the way for their descendants, if the Zhou had lasted longer. One was father to a king. Four war-lords, but for all their similarities four very different characters. Their stories gain depth and drama when taken together, their activities cleverly linked and their characters contrasted.

Yet it is not the lords who stand out most in these four stories on the whole. The most vivid characters are more often than not their retainers, men sometimes of the lowest social rank – burglar, farmyard impersonator, shabby Feng Huan, obscure Mao Sui, down-and-out recluse Hou Ying. And one of the lords is further put in the shade by

---

[1] See Griffith, S. B. *Sun Tzu: The Art of Warfare*, Oxford 1963, Foreword p. xi.

HISTORICAL INTRODUCTION

Yu the Grand Vizier, who in spite of his lofty title is also of humble origin.

In Sima Qian's section on the Assassins there are five might-be assassins, but only two actually kill their man. Two of the others are killed themselves. The longest and most gripping story concerns an attempt that tragically failed. Clearly success was no criterion in Sima Qian's choice of these tales. In fact he is no more recommending assassination here than he is recommending war when he portrays strategists. The situation of violence provides the setting for drama and for the exposition of a particular code of conduct. It is as well to dwell for a moment on this last point. In the unsettled times of the Warring States, it became difficult to pick out friend or foe by conventional judgments on the basis of status, external appearance, or conduct, and very important to be able to recognise a kindred spirit by more subtle and inspired means. For a ruler it became all-important to be able to recognise ability and loyalty, and for an ordinary man with ambition it became all-important to be recognised for one's good qualities. The obligation to achieve fame was a strong one in ancient China in general. Fame was viewed as the necessary external complement to inner virtue. One owed a great deal to someone who furthered one's chances of achieving one's due fame. A superior who recognised one's true great worth and treated one accordingly with honour and friendship was deserving of the utmost loyalty and gratitude. One was morally obliged to try and repay him. Since his very ability to recognise one's value implied that he was a kindred spirit whose existential aims resembled one's own, it was the more natural to help him to further those aims. This "true friendship" was a complex notion and requires to be considered amidst the chaos of the Warring States for a true understanding of its urgency.

Chaos. . . . Yes, certainly. There was a wide-spread conviction that unification was the natural or desirable state of affairs for China: and until that was achieved things were bound to seem unstable and provisional. At the same time, historians tend to overlook certain solidities and thus to reduce the momentousness of the struggles. It should be remembered that some of the States were vast areas with huge populations, bigger than many medieval European states. They were able to muster armies that were enormous for any age. Some of the States, moreover, endured for hundreds of years, longer than most imperial dynasties in China. Political consciousness of empire-wide problems was high, producing correspondingly high tensions. The assassinations should be viewed against this momentous background. The last attempted assassination is one of the most tantalising ifs of all time. If the attempt had succeeded, it might well have done Qin power irreparable harm. The psychological and prestige effects would have been immense. All the more dramatically, it was an attempt at the eleventh hour.

The last section of stories is about Jesters, men of wit and humour who were as influential at times as many grimmer and more earnest personalities. They served under autocratic rulers. It is a never-ending source of surprise how ready the monarchs of the Warring States were to lend an ear to philosophers and nonentities, even to endure great insolence when it meant receiving good advice. The high cultural levels and the premiums placed on ability partly explain this. All the same, the monarchs were also very violent men, who could be horrifically harsh towards advisers. In such situations, it is very often only humour that can approach without disaster. It was very difficult to order a man's decapitation just after he had made one laugh. Difficult to stand on the high-horse of inviolable majesty after having had one's leg pulled! The court jester in ancient China had much the same function as he often had in ancient European courts. His entertaining folly was also expected to embody wisdom when the need arose. Humour is in some ways the finest form of human thinking and often the most suited for delicate situations. Yet who but Sima Qian would have thought fit to include a section on jokesters in a grand history of the world?

The Jesters take us slightly beyond the Zhou, through the Qin Dynasty, and on into the first few years of the Han. It is delightfully ironical to see a court fool piercing the guard of the fearsome First Emperor of the Qin where assassins and generals had all failed.

HISTORICAL INTRODUCTION

It will be noticed that not only are all the chapters saga-woven, with the same characters making an entrance in several of them and with events frequently interlinked, but that there is often a very effective dramatic organisation of the stories within the chapter. The tales of Assassins are arranged chronologically. They are very tightly organised, with a gradual build-up from short curtain-raisers to more and more elaborate and exciting tales, culminating in by far the longest and most striking. Sima Qian provides several layers of story. Each tale is a whole in itself, yet the impact of each is deepened by its setting within the chapter, within the period, and within the whole drama of the age. Each is best appreciated if one bears all the layers simultaneously in mind.

Sima Qian's style in the original Chinese is brilliantly flexible. Sometimes he gallops like a runaway horse. Sometimes he minces like a girl on a tightrope. In tense action his phrases jerk out in brief, violent punches. When summing up a delicate and involved matter he can be a juggler balancing all the furniture in the house at once. Sometimes he uses incredibly involved sentences, hewn-out rough and leaving one breathless at the end of them. Some people have attributed this and other supposed faults to the haste with which he had to compile his history. A closer look, however, shows that scarcely a word is ever wasted, that nearly everything connects up sooner or later with the purpose of the story. Sima Qian writes with economy and power. The long passages of elaborate, heavy intrigue are fascinating to savour in themselves, but provide a startlingly effective foil for the sudden crashing-in of *staccato* action. A good deal of what he writes must of course reflect his sources, but we know that he sometimes paraphrased these to suit his own style.

In our translations we use the system of romanisation known as "Pinyin". This is neater, we feel, than the apostrophe-ridden Wade-Giles system, and is nowadays being more and more widely used. There is a State normally romanised Han. To avoid confusion with the Han of "Han Dynasty" we romanise the State as Hân. Likewise there are two States normally romanised as Wei. One of these we give as Wey. As these stories are intended for a general non-specialist public, we have reduced the density of faceless romanisation by translating some of the proper names, though this is not a universally accepted practice. The stories are sometimes fairly packed with place and personal names and titles. Transliterating all of them sometimes produces a monotonous, confused picture and conceals much colour. In many cases they are vivid nicknames or place-names whose meaning would have been quite clear to the Chinese. We have translated a fair number of them, with the general exception of surnames and male personal names. But we adopt no hard and fast line on this. Where a name is nowadays well known in a romanised form, we leave it as such. Similarly where we have not been able to provide an easy or vivid translation of a name, we have resorted to romanisation. Tracing etymologies of ancient Chinese names is notoriously hazardous. We do not claim perfection, only to aim at liveliness. It will be an easy matter for any expert to check or rectify with the original Chinese text.

As an aid to the sense of awe that the vastness of time can inspire and as a help in locating events, we have included a number of regnal dates, hoping that this will not offend or disturb. We enclose them in square brackets. They may also serve to facilitate situational connexions between the stories. These dates are given according to Wan Guoding's *Zhongguo lishi jinianbiao*, Hong Kong 1958.

In translating and understanding Sima Qian we are indebted to all who have written on him before. The patient work of numerous Chinese and Japanese annotators and editors has lightened our work and we would also like to pay tribute to various Western scholars. Edouard Chavannes with his *Mémoirs historiques de Se-ma Ts'ien*, 5 vols., 1895 – 1905, laid the massive foundations for Western studies of Sima Qian. Above all

HISTORICAL INTRODUCTION

we are grateful to the modern master Burton Watson for his various studies on the *Historical Records*, in particular his *Ssu-ma Ch'ien: Grand Historian of China* (Columbia University Press 1958), the most thorough-going picture of Sima Qian and his work. Our faults are all very much our own.

Edinburgh
March 1973   WILLIAM DOLBY

Literary and Critical Introduction
Sima Qian's contribution to fiction and romance

To many it may seem something of a paradox to link the Father of Chinese Historiography with History's bastard bairns – story-telling and fiction. Yet as a great literary historian and creator of the *vitae* and portraits of individual characters, Sima, like Carlyle, saw these

> *in the most important sense more true than the cold analysis of the same events and the conventional summings up of the same persons by scientific historians who, with more knowledge of facts, have less understanding of Man.*[1]

God save us from scientific historians! The Grand Historian may be responsible for the formal structure of later official dynastic histories, but in no way can he be blamed for their frequently boring contents and incredibly tepid narrative technique. A recent scientific historian went out of his way to vindicate Judge Jeffreys, suggesting, nay proving, that he was no whit more severe in his sentencing than any other seventeenth-century justice. This may well be the case, and the defence rests. But for my money I prefer Macaulay's unscientific portrait of the old monster. Similarly Sima described the First Emperor of the Qin, a book-burner and dictator, as having a face like a scorpion. Recent Marxist historians in China would rather have us pay heed to his contribution to the "march of progress", and ignore his remarkably unscientific phizog. They have a point, too. But I still prefer the wonderfully awesome and strikingly sinister description of Sima. Strangely enough, both new schools of scientific history detract from the majesty of their subjects. Thanks to Sima Qian and Macaulay both His Imperial Majesty Qin Shi-Huang and Lord Justice Jeffreys have on the one

---

[1] G. M. Trevelyan, Clio a Muse, quoted by A. Marwick, *The Nature of History*, London (Macmillan) 1970, p. 57.

hand incurred the opprobium of later generations for their cold-blooded cruelty but on the other preserved an undying respect for simply being "great historical personalities". I am equally sure that both villains would much rather stand out as peers in the realm of cruelty than just be relegated to the same level as lesser jurists and monarchs.

How much the more likable, in one sense, is the machinating "Corporal John", thieving from his mistresses, rigging his military campaigns like a dirty football fixture list, as he appears in Thackeray's *History of Henry Esmond*, than His Grace the Duke of Marlborough in Winston Churchill's rather heavy number – despite its diligent use of family archives. Here one has to agree with John Sutherland that

the opinion of Winston Churchill, the official biographer of Marlborough, that Macaulay is a liar and Henry Esmond, in this respect, "malicious" should perhaps be appended to any edition.[2]

Just as Macaulay gave birth to Thackeray, Sima gave birth to the great Chinese picaresque tradition of fiction-writing.

When Sima Qian juxtaposed the Four War-Lords, he envisaged a saga or novel within his History. The four lords were to be the coigns of the Warring States Period from which could be seen the deeds of derring-do of cat-burglars, dog-butchers, down-at-heel scholars – a vast panorama of assorted retainers. All of which he referred to as *you-xia* – a term nicely translated by James Liu[3] as Knight Errants, but for which we at some times prefer "wandering swashbucklers" and at others "villains". The Four War-Lords are, then, in Sima Qian's description, simply vehicles for an examination of men who would otherwise have "perished as though they had never been."

---

[2] J. Sutherland "A Note on Thackeray as Historian", in W. M. Thackeray *The History of Henry Esmond*, Harmondsworth (Penguin) 1970.

[3] J. J. W. Liu, *The Chinese Knight Errant*, London (Routledge & Kegan Paul) 1967.

As to the plain, russet-coated captains of olden times – we haven't any information handed down. More recently there have been the followers of the Prince of Yen Ling[4] and those of the Four War-Lords, Lord Mengchang, Lord Great Plain, Lord Trust Tumulus, and Lord Chunshen of Chu. These princes and lords were all of the royal blood and relied on their landed wealth and superior station to gather the world's worthy and able men about themselves, thus acquiring a reputation amongst the feudal lords. I do not suggest that they themselves were not likewise worthy and able, but that they rode on the reputation of their humble clients and retainers. They were like wind-shouters – for it was not the force of the shout but rather the speed of the wind that blazed their reputation. Yet there were their followers, the back-street swashbucklers who got a grip on themselves, and loved the cause so that their repute was world renowned – there was not one among such men who was not worthy. Theirs, I might say, was indeed a difficult doings. Nonetheless, the intellectual Confucians and do-gooding Mohists have pushed these plebian knights aside and never accorded them recorded mention.

So writes Sima in his introduction to the *Swashbucklers' Vitae*,[5] in praise not of famous men, princes and leaders, but reserving his greatest admiration for the "plebian knight errants". Men similar in temperament and stature to Lord Mengchang's extraordinary clients – Feng Huan the rent-book-burner, the cat-burglar, the farmyard-noise-impersonator, the porter, and the dog-butcher. It is thus that Sima set the pattern for the heroes of heterodox fiction and created the great tradition of the "popular knight errant". A tradition beloved, not so much by the Confucian bureaucratic establishment, as by bohemian

---

[4] Wang Boxiang, who follows the commentaries of Liang Yusheng and Zhang Wenhu, considers that, since the Prince of Yen Ling, Ji Zha, kept no retainers or clients, his insertion here is probably a later textual interpolation: see Wang Boxiang, *Shi Ji Xuan*, Peking (Ren-min Wen-xue Chu-ban-she) 1958, p. 492.

[5] *Yu-xia lie-zhuan*, *Shi-ji*, *Shiki kaichuu kooshoo*, ed. Takikawa Kametaroo.

LITERARY AND CRITICAL INTRODUCTION

poets and writers such as Li Bo, who lived out his swashbuckling fantasies in real life, getting fighting drunk, beating up local bullies, and even doing a spot of "righteous killing".

In the Golden Age of popular fiction-writing, the Ming Dynasty (1368–1644), dramatists, novelists, and short-story writers took the *you-xia* tradition of the *Historical Records* as manifested in the War-Lords and Assassins for their model. Not only did they borrow their heroes from these accounts of Sima, they even created new characters from popular traditions whose life-styles and heroic actions were inspired by this section of *The Historical Records*.

In the greatest of all China's picaresque novels – the *Shui Hu Zhuan* or *Fenland Saga* – the thirty-six leading bandits are befriended at various times by certain *Yuan-wai, da-guan-ren*, or Squires.[6] The literary prototypes to these broad-minded members of the gentry are none other than our old friends Lord Mengchang, Lord Flat Plain, Lord Trust Tumulus, and Lord Chunshen of Chu.

In the third chapter of the *Fenland Saga*, an illiterate captain of the guard called Lu Da has come to the aid of a poor itinerant singing-girl and her father. The singing-girl was being put upon by a local pork-butcher known as the Guanxi Crusher. Infuriated by the fact that underworld travelling people were being oppressed by a rich bully, Captain Lu went off and beat the living breath out of the Guanxi Crusher – a pork-butcher, and no dog-butcher, he. Fleeing for his life, Captain Lu is later befriended by a Squire Zhao. Through Squire Zhao's well-meant but somewhat misplaced services, Lu, the good hearted roughneck, becomes an altogether indifferent member of the Buddhist priesthood. Before long the erstwhile Captain Lu (now known as the Tattooed Monk) has broken practically all the vows in the *sutras*. He gets roaring drunk, forces dog-meat down the throats of his more pious brethren, smashes the *vajras* or sacred-gate god-images, beats up not a

---

[6] Shui-hu Zhuan [The Fenland Saga]. This novel is also referred to as *All Men are Brothers* (the title of Pearl S. Buck's translation), and as *The Water Margins* (the title of Jackson's translation).

few of his fellow monks, shits and pisses within the holy precincts, and generally lets himself down with incredible and inimitable style. Yet he remains a leading character in the novel – protector of the weak and mighty deflator of pompous phonies. Whereas Squire Zhao, the equivalent of one of Sima's war-lords, having completed his function of giving the humble Lu more adventurous scope, soon disappears from the narrative scene.

A more important foil than Squire Zhao is Chai Jin, or Squire Chai, who in the ninth chapter befriends another key character from the lower orders – Lin (Leopard's Head) Chong, one time Garrison Arms Instructor. After having served his purpose of introducing Lin Chong, Squire Chai turns up again in the twenty-fifth chapter, when he befriends the brigands' leader Song (Timely Rain) Jiang. Lest there remain any doubt as to his link with the war-lord tradition, consider the following:

'I've heard tell,' replied Song Qing, 'in underworld circles that there's a gentleman of Meng Hai Command in the Cang Zhou region by the name of Squire Chai. They say he's a direct lateral descendant of Emperor Da Zhou. Though I've never had the honour of being introduced to him, why don't we go and trust in his good hospitality? They tell me he's a lover of honour and a good spender. Devoted, that's what he is, to making friends with the world's fine fellows – the good men and true, you might say. He'll always help out any poor convict man. In fact you might call him a regular latter-day Lord Mengchang. All we've got to do is pay him a call.'[7]

At the end of the same chapter Song Jiang, the future leader of the band, whilst at Squire Chai's house, literally runs into yet another member of the outlaws, Wu (Ganger) Song.[8] Thereafter in the novel

---

[7] *Shui-hu*, Peking (Ren-min Wen-xue Chu-ban-she) 1972, p. 251.
[8] Wu Xing-zhe, lit. Wu the Walker. I have called him 'Ganger', so as to link up with Ganger Hrolf, the Icelandic saga hero.

LITERARY AND CRITICAL INTRODUCTION

Little Lord Meng Chang[9] fades into the background and leaves the stage for the true heroes, "the plebeian knight errants", Song (the Timely Rain) Yu, Wu (Ganger) Song, Lu (Tattoed Priest), Ling (Leopard's Head) Chong, and their rumbustious companions. He does, however, reappear in the fifty-second chapter, when he is arrested by the corrupt mandarin Gao Lian and later rescued at the eleventh hour by Li (Black Whirlwind) Kui, Squire Chai then joins the rebel band, in which he is accorded honourable position and rank, but plays no further part in the action until the final chapter where he is listed as the eighteenth of the thirty-six heroes, and referred to as Chai (Little Whirlwind) Jin – no longer as a *da guan-ren*, or squire, but simply another "plebeian knight errant". Though he has gone up in the underworld, his name has been struck from the Chinese equivalent of Douglas's *Retours* or Burke's *Peerage*.

It is not surprising that the late Ming literary critic Jin Shengtan, an outstanding bohemian and courageous outsider, whose edition *The Fenland Saga* has remained the popular version till today, should have listed Sima Qian's *Historical Records* and the *Fenland Saga* together amongst the world's few books of "remarkable talent".[10] Such opinion had also been shared by earlier heterodox *literati* of the late Ming. As Professor James Liu remarks in his definitive of Chinese Knight Errantry,

> Shui Hu Zhuan (The Fenland Saga) *has long been recognized as a masterpiece. Even in days when fiction was not considered serious literature in China, a few literary men esteemed it highly. The famous poet and essayist Yuan Hongdao (1568–1610) mentioned Luo Guanzhong, its alleged author, in the same breath as the great historian and acknowledged*

---

[9] In the Jin-ping-mei Chi-hua, Chai Jin is also referred to as Xiao Mengchang, or Little Lord Mengchang.

[10] Chen Dong-yuan, *Jin Shengtan Zhuan*, Hong Kong (Xiang-gang Taiping Shu-ju Yin-hang) 1963.

master of classical prose Sima Qian, and the critics Li Zhi (1527 – 1602) and Jing Shengtan both placed the romance among the greatest works of genius in Chinese literature.[11]

If the later romance-writers reversed the primacy of the roles of warlords and retainers in such works as the *Fenland Saga*, they were sticking to the spirit of the *Historical Records*. For Sima Qian very much regrets that –

As to the plain, russet-coated captains of olden times – we have no information handed down.[12]

Yet, although he was hampered by inadequate source materials he did not allow the allied demands of the scientific historian to handicap him when he created a deal of lively (presumably unscientific) dialogue for such men as Feng Xuan (or Feng Huan) in Lord Mengchang's *Vita*.

An even more vivid example of the influence which the *Historical Records* exerted on *you-xia* fiction-writers is the case of Ling Mengchu (1580 – 1644). James Liu has mentioned Ling's dramas, but strangely enough ignored his most outstanding short story "The Adventures of Lazy Dragon, the Master Burglar of Soochow".[13] Master Ling starts his story with a *ru-hua*, or introductory narrative, devoted to a flash-back of Lord Mengchang's two unorthodox retainers – the burglar, and the farmyard-noise-impersonator. Then before embarking on the deeds of Lazy Dragon he makes a facetious jibe at the Confucianised civil service examinations as a means of selecting worthy men for public office. In describing Lazy Dragon, this extraordinary magistrate and man of letters, Ling Meng-chu sums up the thief's accomplishments in verse:

---

[11] Liu, *The Chinese Knight Errant*.
[12] Liu, *op. cit*.
[13] Ling Mengchu, *The Lecherous Academician and Other Tales*, tr. John Scott, London (André Deutsch) forthcoming.

LITERARY AND CRITICAL INTRODUCTION

So limber that he seems to have no bones,
His footsteps pass more silent than a sigh,
He strides across the roof-beams like a giant
Or walks up walls, as tiny as a fly.

All situations he can play by ear,
Or, if need be, can shape his supple lips
To mimic cat or dog or rat; and all
Deceptive sounds are at his finger tips.

His mimicry is truer than the truth;
Just like a ghost he flits, now there, now here,
Quick as a gust of wind, a shower of rain;
In all the underworld he has no peer.

If twentieth-century western sophisticates complain that such extraordinary talents offend against the demands of "social realism", may I point out in defence of Master Ling (and Lazy Dragon, for that matter) that China and Japan have long had their underworld equivalents of Mr Alfie Hines? The Japanese have a special term borrowed from Chinese tradition for the arts of escapology, wall-scaling, tunnelling, impersonations, animal-noise mimicry, and other demanding requirements expected of a master thief. It is called NINJUTSU. James Bond learned about this incredible oriental invention in his adventures in Japan in a work of fiction far less realistic, as its title suggests, than that of Lazy Dragon – *You Only Live Twice.*

Undoubtedly Sima Qian made original and somewhat irregular use of the source-materials available to him. J. I. Crump points out in his introduction to *The Intrigues of the Warring States:*

It is only sensible to assume that Sima Qian did his best to acquire and sift all the information on the past available to him when he wrote the Shi Ji *(Historical Records). With this in mind it is perfectly clear that the period of history generally known as the Era of the Warring States (traditionally*

453 – 221 B.C.) *yields, for Sima Qian the historian, a very unsatisfactory amount and kind of historical raw material: "For the forces and changes of the Warring States, there are texts which can be put together – but how is one to be sure that they are of any antiquity?"* [See E. Chavannes, Les Memoires historiques de Se-ma Ts'ien, *Paris* 1895 – 1905, 5/3, 3/27.] . . . *It is almost a certainty that the source which allowed Sima Qian to write eleven separate biographies of prominent men of the Warring States, rich in details of speech and deed, was the* Intrigues of the Warring States.[14]

I certainly would not have the temerity to cast any doubt on Professor Crump's initial assumption that one of Sima Qian's sources must almost certainly have been the *Intrigues*. But the only extant version of the *Intrigues* which has been transmitted to us is that which Liu Xiang edited c. 8 B.C.; and, if Sima Qian used any similar version, a comparison of its account of the episode involving Mengchang's retainer Feng Huang (also known as Feng Xuan) with his suggests that he must not only have made a considerable expansion of the dramatic dialogue, but must also have added various subtle changes of narrative emphasis and innuendo.

Here is the version contained in the *Intrigues*:

A man of Qi, one Feng Xuan, being in a most impoverished condition, sent a mediary to Lord Mengchang to inform him that he wished to become a retainer.

'What is the gentleman partial to?' asked Lord Mengchang.
'He has no partiality,' was the reply.
'What is he especially capable of ? '
'Nothing.'
Lord Mengchang laughed. 'So be it,' he said, and admitted him.
From this Lord Mengchang's attendants assumed that their Lord held the

---

[14] See J. I. Crump jr, *The Intrigues*, University of Michigan Press, 1964, intro., p. ix.

new retainer in low esteem and supplied him with only coarse fare. After a time he appeared, leaning against a pillar, tapping on his unsheathed longsword and singing: 'Longsword, let us return! We find no fish on our plate.' When his attendants reported this to Lord Mengchang, he told them to make Feng Xuan's fare that of his other retainers.

Shortly thereafter, Feng Xuan again sang his sword song: 'Longsword, let us return! No carriage to ride in state!' The attendants laughed at him and reported it to Lord Mengchang.

'Have a conveyance made, the equal of those who have carriages,' he replied.

Thereafter Feng Xuan would ride in his carriage with his sword over his shoulder and passing his friends, would say:

'Longsword, let us return. No support, can my family wait?'

The attendants all disliked him then, for they thought him covetous and malcontent.

'Does he have a family?' asked Lord Mengchang.

'His mother,' they replied.

So Lord Mengchang dispatched a man to supply her needs so that she might not want. Feng Xuan never sang his sword song again.

Afterwards, Lord Mengchang inscribed a notice asking his retainers, 'Who among you can keep accounts and will collect the monies owed me in my fief of Xue?'

Feng Xuan sent in his reply, 'I can.'

Lord Mengchang was curious and asked who he was. His attendants told him that it was he who sang the song of the longsword.

'So he has capabilities after all!' laughed Lord Mengchang. 'But I have neglected him and never given him audience.'

When Lord Mengchang received Feng Xuan, he apologized and said: 'I have been much busied by affairs and vexed with troubles so that my feelings are blunted. Deep in affairs of state, I have wronged you; yet you, sir, take no offence and are willing to collect debts for me in Xue?'

'I am.'

When Feng Xuan had made ready his attire and loaded the waggons with debt-tallies he took leave of Lord Mengchang.

'When the debts have been collected, is there anything I may buy for you when I return?' he asked.

'If you have seen something that my house lacks, buy it,' replied Lord Mengchang.

Feng Xuan hastened to Xue and sent an officer summoning all those who owed debts to come forth and match their tallies. When all had been matched, Feng Xuan feigned an order from Lord Mengchang that all debts were to be forgiven the people. The tallies were burned and the people cheered.

Feng Xuan returned to Qi without a halt and arrived in the early morning asking audience. Lord Mengchang, surprised at his haste, donned his formal robes and admitted him.

'Why do you return so speedily? Have the debts been collected?'

'They have already been collected,' was the reply.

'What did you purchase on your return?'

'My lord, you asked me to see if there was anything your house lacked,' answered Feng Xuan. 'It was my humble opinion that your castle was filled with precious objects, that your stables and kennels abounded in steeds and coursers, and the lower palaces with beauties. It seemed that one thing only was lacking, and that was fealty. This I bought, my lord.'

'How can one buy fealty?' exclaimed Lord Mengchang.

'At the moment you hold the little fief of Xue; you do not cherish the people there as your own children, but look on them as a source of profit,' replied Feng Xuan. 'Your servant took it upon himself to feign an order from you that all debts should be forgiven the people of Xue. The tallies were burned and the citizens cheered you. This is how your servant purchased fealty.'

Lord Mengchang was displeased. 'So be it! You may now rest, sir.' [15]

The last sentence (which reads in Chinese *Menchang Jun bu yue, yue; nuo, xian-sheng xiu yi*) might just as well be translated: "Lord Meng-

---

[15] J. I. Crump jr, *Chan-kuo Ts'e*, Oxford (Clarendon Press) 1970.

chang was not amused. 'Very well, sir,' he said, 'why don't you take a holiday?' "

In Sima Qian's version of the initial interview between Feng Huan and Lord Mengchang there is a marked echo in the dialogue of that between the Confucian philosopher Mencius and King Hui of Liang in the opening of the *Book of Mencius*.

When Mencius was granted an audience by King Hui of Liang, the King said:
   'Old man, you do not consider a thousand li too far to come here. What is that you bring of profit to my kingdom?'
   'Why must your majesty talk of profit?' replied Mencius. 'There are also benevolence and fealty – that is enough.' [16]

Compare this with Sima's "parody":

An earlier incident in the life of Lord Mengchang involves Feng Huan, who had heard that Lord Mengchang was keen on gathering together clients and retainers, and went for an interview with him, turning up for it in shabby straw sandals.
   'Venerable sir,' said Lord Mengchang, 'you've humbled yourself to come so far to see me. What learned counsels have you to offer me?'
   'Well, my lord.' said Feng, 'I've just heard you're fond of the company of fine men, and being hard up myself, I've come along to offer my services.'

It should be remembered that Sima Qian was writing at the time when Confucianism was starting its long reign as the state-blessed orthodox credo. Though Sima admired the Sage and scholars of the past he had undoubted reservations about their self-appointed legatees, his contemporary courtier officials and sycophants. In this section he appears to be parodying Confucius's St Paul, Mencius, with the more

---

[16] Opening lines of Mencius, *Shi-shu*.

lovable common swashbuckler Feng Huan, whilst at the same time making a good humoured contrast between King Hui [Magnaminity] and the true aristocrat Lord Mengchang.

This use of irony, more to be expected in a romance than a straight history – particularly as the whole nature of the interview seems to be an inspired fabrication – is reinforced by the later excuse to which Feng Huan offers Lord Mengchang after he has burnt the tallies, and when he explains that he has thus prevented his lord from acquiring the reputation of being "a ruler who loves profit, lacking in any affection for your gentry and people".

"A ruler who loves profit [*jun hao li*]" is once again a direct echo of Mencius. We cannot help suspecting that the Grand Historian is looking back nostalgically to the simple plebeian knights of the immediate but totally different past, and subconsciously contrasting their honest bluffness and plain-speaking with the sycophantic yapping of the Confucian bureaucrats and pen-pushing courtiers of his own age, cowardly men who held more responsible for his own terrible emasculation than Emperor Han Wu Di, the Martial.

Certainly it is the same spirit which made Ling Mengchu create his housebreaker hero Lazy Dragon, and talk of the cat-burglar and farmyard-noise-impersonator:

Now Lord Mengchang had formerly patronised a whole host of retainers and clients: but when he escaped from Qin it was entirely due to the efforts of these two humble men. A point which proves that no man's talent, however lowly, should ever be despised. Yet nowadays those in high places lay undue emphasis on the Official Service Examination; and unless a fellow has been through that rat-race, no matter how fantastic his talents, he has no hope of making a government career for himself. That's why a good many clever lads with dodgy and naughty skills, finding themselves up against the system, are forced to embark on a life of crime.[17]

---

[17] Ling Mengchu, *Er-ke Pai-an Jing-qi*, Taibei (Shi-jie Shu-ju Yin-hang) 1968, Vol. III.

LITERARY AND CRITICAL INTRODUCTION

Again, in the *Vita* of Mengchang, Sima forges a facetious link between staid and proper Confucius and Mencius and the delightful War-Lord's colourful retinue, when in his closing commentary he states;

I once passed through the Marshgrass region. It is common in the villages and small towns there to encounter whole gangs of violent young fellows. In this respect it is quite different from the neighbouring regions of Zou and Lu. *I enquired about the reason behind the violence prevalent in this area. Lord Mengchang, I was told, brought wandering swashbucklers and villains from all over the world flocking into Marshgrass till they and their dependants numbered more than sixty thousand. Historical records tell us that Lord Mengchang delighted in the pastime of collecting clients. A reputation well earned, I would suggest!*

Now Zou and Lu were the birth places of Mencius and Confucius respectively. The geographical juxtaposition heightens the contrast between the two groups, the Confucians and the Swashbucklers. This reference in his Grand Historian's Commentary is a symbolic interpolation, and probably quite unscientifically sound when one considers the number of years separating Sima Qian's generation from Lord Mengchang's.

In this, one of his finest sections of the *Historical Records*, Sima appears more Taoist in temperament than an orthodox Confucian. But this is a hazardous point to pursue, since, like all truly universal writers, he refuses to slip conveniently into any particular ready-made pigeonhole.

Whatever Sima's attitude towards Confucianism and its opposite number Taoism, Tang Shunzhi (1507 – 1560), or Tang Ying-de, a well-known Confucian mandarin discerned dangerous and subversive precedents, sixteen hundred years later, in the *Vitae* of the section of his Historical Records which Sima devoted to the War-Lords. Tang was writing in the heyday of romances and popular literary activity. All such reading-matter would have been anathema to any such "upright Confucian" who saw within it the germ of rebellion and political disorder. Tang saw fit to write a famous essay criticising Prince Fearless of Wei, Lord Trust Tumulus. His contention is that the glorification of Trust Tumulus and his retainers had encouraged later generations to hatch anti-establishment sects and factions and to take up arms against the legitimate ruling house. Of Trust Tumulus he says:

Even within the King's seraglio there was his favourite who knew it was Prince Fearless who counted in the nation – not the King. Outside in the neighbouring Kingdom of Zhao the people looked up to Trust Tumulus – but not the legitimate monarch. Amongst the common people there was the Wild Man of the Barbarian Gate (Hou Ying) and he too recognised Trust Tumulus as his leader – but not the King. ... Alas, from then onwards there has been a decline in moral standards. People are for ever forming death-defying secret cliques and suicide factions, determined to defy the interests of the ruler and putting themselves in defiance of the commonweal. ... Men such as the itinerant swashbuckler Vizier Yu recognised the friendship of plain, russet-coated captains, but denied their duty to the Monarch. So it has come about that frequently the Monarch has become naught but a figure-head – a pendant tassle of an empty crown.[18]

In the last sentence but one Tang, by his reference to Vizier Yu and his allusion to bu-yi [plain, russet-coated men], the phrase used by Sima in the introduction to his *Vitae* of the Swashbucklers, makes it clear enough that his concern is not with one isolated war-lord, Trust Tumulus, but rather with the larger popular tradition, the whole gamut of *you-xia* or plebeian knight-errantry.

In fairness to Tang and the Confucian tradition, if we absent ourselves the while from fiction and return to pure history, it is only too true that the Chinese body politic has been plagued throughout its history with a surfeit of war-lords. Their lives may make for a good read, but

---

[18] Tang Shunzhi, *Xin-ling Jun Jiu Zhao Lun*, in *Gu-wen Guan-zhi*, Taibei (San-min Shu-ju Yin-hang) 1971.

LITERARY AND CRITICAL INTRODUCTION

in stark reality to be alive with them was often a hazardous business. The Chinese have always been great ones for *zhi-shang tan bing* – "discussing war on paper".

With its proletarian heroes one would have expected Chinese Communism to have made a great thing of the *you-xia* tradition, but it seems to have died the death. Perhaps the government of the People's Republic has taken Tang Shunzhi's criticism to heart. Nonetheless leafing through a little picture book from China called *Di-dao Zhan*[19] or Tunnel Warfare I was amazed to see that one of the leading communist guerilla heroes in this tale from the Anti-Japanese War was Zhao Ping-yuan – Flat Plain Zhao. Can this be a subconscious reference to our old friend Lord Flat Plain of Zhao, the most pusillanimous and least attractive of the four war-lords?

At all events, Sima Qian's fans will all be pleased to know that his temple has been restored in the last few years. According to *New Archaelogical Finds in China*, Peking (Foreign Languages Press) 1972,

another well-preserved historical site is the Temple to Sima Qian.... Sima, famous historian and man of letters of the Han Dynasty, wrote the first Chinese general history Shi Ji [Historical Records]. *... Teng Shih-yu, caretaker of the historical site since 1958, is a former Red Army soldier who was disabled.*

However, it does go on to tell us:

He (Teng Shih-yu) has turned the temple into a "school" for propagating Mao Tse-tung's thought and giving class education.

The scope and technique of Sima Qian and his heirs, the writers of fiction and historical romances has much in common with that of the

---

[19] *Di-dao Zhan*, Peking (Ren-min Mei-shu Chu-ban-she) 1972.

great Icelandic saga-writers. It is not just the name that makes Ganger Hrolf so akin to Wu (Walker) Song in the *Fenland Saga*. Their values and adventures have a remarkable similarity. There is little doubt that Sima would have heartily agreed with the anonymous fourteenth-century Icelandic romantic historian who wrote:

If people want to listen to old stories, they ought first of all to bear in mind that most sagas are made up of certain specific materials. Some are about God and his holy men, and from these a good deal of wisdom can be gained, though the Lives of the Saints don't give many people very much entertainment.[20]

And that is precisely why we have not included the *vitae* immediately preceding that of Mengchang and his band – *The Lives of the Philosophers: Mencius and Xun Qing.*

Edinburgh 1973   JOHN SCOTT

---

[20] Hermann Pálsson, *Islendinga Sagakemmtun*, tr. H. Pálsson & P. Edwards; also H. Pálsson & P. Edwards, *Legendary Fiction in Medieval Iceland*, Studia Islandica, Reukjavík (University of Iceland: Faculty of Liberal Arts) 1970, p. 37.

STRATEGISTS

Sun the Martial

MASTER SUN THE MARTIAL originated from the Kingdom of Chu. On the merit of his treatise on *The Arts of War* he gained an audience with Helu, King of Wu [514 – 496].

'I have carried out a thorough examination of your thirteen chapters on warfare, Master Sun,' said King Helu. 'Now, would you favour me with a small demonstration of how you exercise actual command over troops?'

'Certainly,' replied Sun the Martial.

'And could the demonstration be conducted with women?'

'Yes, indeed.'

So the King permitted a display. Sun the Martial took one hundred and eighty palace ladies from the King's seraglio, and these he divided into two half-companies to be commanded by the King's favourite concubines, whom he appointed to wield the halberds of warrant.

'Don't you know your front, left, right, and rear?' were his first words.

'We do, sir,' they replied.

'On the order "Face your front" you will face me. On "Left turn" you will face left. On "Right turn" you will face right. And on the order "About turn" you will turn about and face your rear.'

'Very good, sir,' replied the ladies.

After familiarising them with his system of military discipline, he had the axes of martial law set up on display and repeatedly dinned into them the instructions and penalties for disobedience. But as soon as the kettle-drums beat 'Right turn' the women just burst into laughter.

'If the rules of discipline are not clarified and the troops not familiarised with commands, then the general is at fault,' Master Sun announced.

Once more he dinned into them the instructions and penalties for disobedience, then had the kettle-drums signal 'Left turn'. Still the women just burst into laughter.

'Well,' said Master Sun, 'if the rules of discipline are not clarified and the troops not familiarised with the commands, the general is at fault.

When these things *have* been clarified and orders are still not complied with, then it is the warrant officers who are at fault.'

He was just about to have the half-company sergeants beheaded, when the King looking down from his observation terrace was suddenly horrified to see both his beloved concubines about to suffer execution and hastily despatched a messenger to try and countermand the order.

'His Majesty is now fully aware of your skill in the arts of warfare, General,' explained the messenger, 'but without these favourites life for His Majesty would be as food lacking flavour. He would prefer you to spare their heads.'

'I have already received my ruler's mandate of command.' Master Sun replied, 'and once a general is in operational control of his army there are occasions when he may ignore his ruler's whim and fancy.'

So saying, he executed both sergeants as a warning to the others and replaced them by the next two in line. Once again the drums sounded. Now the women moved to the right and left, advanced and retreated, knelt and rose with faultless precision. No-one dared so much as utter a sound.

Sun now sent a messenger to report back to the King. 'Your troops are all in perfect battle array, awaiting Your Majesty's inspection. Whatever it is your wish to command them, be it to have them tread fire and water, they will comply.'

'The Commander is free to retire to his quarters: it is not Our pleasure to review troops today,' was the King's reply.

'The King is merely in love with words and shuns realities,' commented Master Sun.

Now that he was aware of Master Sun's military insight, the King eventually made him Commander-in-Chief. In the Western Expedition, when mighty Chu was smashed and its capital, Ying, violated, and again in the northern campaigns when the Kingdoms of Qi and Jin were made to tremble and the fame of the Kingdom of Wu was blazoned among the princes of the world, Master Sun the Martial each time played a powerful role.

Sun the Cripple

MORE THAN A HUNDRED YEARS after the death of Sun the Martial there lived Sun the Cripple. He was born in the region between the cities of Wo and Juan and was a direct descendant of Sun the Martial. At one time he studied the military sciences as a fellow-student of Pang Juan. Later Pang Juan took service in the Kingdom of Wei, where he managed to become a general under King Benevolence [369 – 318]. Knowing that his abilities were inferior to Sun the Cripple's, he secretly sent someone to summon the Cripple to him. After Sun joined him, Pang Juan, was so conscious of his inferiority that he began to harbour jealous feelings towards him: and in the end he concocted legal pretexts for having Sun's legs chopped off and his face branded, so as to ensure that, having shamefully been branded as a common felon, Sun would shun the society of other men.

One day the Ambassador of the Kingdom of Qi came to Daliang, capital of Wei; and Sun the Cripple, forced because he was a punished felon to contrive a secret audience, tried to sell his theories and skills to the Ambassador. Perceiving that he was a remarkable man, the Ambassador hid him in his own chariot and drove with him back to Qi, where General Tian Ji was so impressed by him that he brought him with honour into his own retinue.

Tian Ji often bet heavily with other noblemen on the results of chariot-racing. Master Sun noticed that although there was little difference in speed between the horses that took part, they could still be classed in three main groups; inferior, average, and superior.

'My lord,' he suggested, 'you just go ahead and put down as heavy a stake as you like, and I'll see you win.'

Tian Ji had complete confidence in him and wagered a thousand pieces of gold against the King and the other nobles.

'Match your inferior quadrigae against their best ones, pit your best ones against their average ones, and leave your average ones to compete against their inferior teams,' Master Sun advised him just before the races.

Thus, although Tian Ji lost the first race, he won the other two and ended up by winning a thousand pieces of gold from the King. As a direct consequence of this he introduced Sun to Awesome, King of Qi [356 – 319], who sought his opinions on military strategy and appointed him his personal instructor and strategic commander.

Some time afterwards the Kingdom of Wei attacked the Kingdom of Zhao; and, being hard pressed, Zhao solicited aid from Qi. King Awesome of Qi wished to give Sun the Cripple the supreme command, but he refused it.

'A man whose body has been broken by punishment is hardly suitable for such undertakings,' said Sun.

So the King put Tian Ji in operational command, with Master Sun as strategic commander, to be concealed in a covered baggage-wagon where he could plan the campaign at leisure. Tian Ji wanted to lead their forces straight into Zhao, but Master Sun objected.

'In solving a complex problem like this,' said he, 'you don't unravel tangled silks by crushing them in your fist, nor do you stop a duel by wading in and flailing out right and left. We must avoid a headlong confrontation and hit them where they are wide open. Once their manœuvrability is checked and they no longer have a free hand to continue the offensive against Zhao, they will naturally call off their campaign. Wei is busy attacking Zhao at the moment, so that all its crack troops are deployed to the maximum outside the country in Zhao and only old people and children are left at home. You would be best advised to force-march your armies into Daliang and cut off their lines of communication by occupying their vacated military positions. By so doing you will oblige the armies of Wei to withdraw from Zhao and go back to relieve their own capital. In one such move we would raise the siege in Zhao and do ourselves a good turn by cutting the Kingdom of Wei down to size.'

Tian Ji followed his advice. Sure enough, Wei's troops withdrew from Handan, the capital of Zhao, to join battle with Qi at Cinnamon Hill, in the Kingdom of Wei; and there they were thoroughly routed.

Thirteen years later Wei allied with Zhao to attack the state of Hân which sought aid from Qi. Again Tian Ji was put in command. This time, without any delay, he headed straight for Daliang. When Pang Juan, the commander of the Wei troops, heard of this, he withdrew his armies from Hân and headed back home. By now the armies of Qi had crossed the frontier and were advancing westwards into Wei.

'The soldiers of Zhao, Wei, and Hân are all famed for their ferocity and bravery and despise the men of Qi, as our nation has reputation for cowardice,' said Master Sun to Tian Ji, 'but a good strategist turns such a situation to his own advantage. The *Arts of War* states that an impetuous forced march of forty miles in pursuit of a temporary gain can often cut the commander off from his troops, and that a forced march of twenty miles can result in the arrival of only half the army. Bearing this in mind, now that our forces are penetrating Wei territory, you must tonight set up field kitchens for a hundred thousand men, and tomorrow field kitchens for fifty thousand, and the day after enough for thirty thousand.'

After Pang Juan had marched in their wake for three days, he was in excellent spirits.

'I always knew,' he said, 'that the armies of Qi are made up of cowards – they have only been in our territory for some three days, and already half their officers and men have deserted.'

Accordingly he left behind his infantry and with only his *élite* light brigade pressed on after the enemy, covering a journey of two days in one. In the meantime Master Sun had calculated the speed of Pang's advance and estimated that he would reach Horse Mound that same nightfall. Now the road at Horse Mound passes through a precipitous valley on either side of which are many deep gullies ideally suited for laying troops in ambush. In this valley he had a large tree trimmed and on its white stripped stump the following words inscribed:

UNDER THIS TREE
PANG JUAN
DIED

Then he ordered ten thousand of his crossbow sharpshooters to lie in ambush on each side of the defile and warned them all to loose their quarrels simultaneously when they saw a torch raised some time after dusk.

That night Pang Juan duly arrived at the tree-stump. Seeing that there was writing on the white stripped wood, he had tinder struck to light a torch, but hardly had he finished reading the inscription when the sharpshooters of Qi all opened up with a myriad crossbow bolts, plunging the armies of Wei into great panic and confusion. When Pang Juan realised that his troops were routed and that no stratagem could save him he uttered the words, 'Thus have I made a name for that witless runt,' and cut his own throat. The armies of Qi followed up their victory by completely smashing the enemy and capturing Crown Prince Shen of Wei, whom they took back as a hostage. So it was that Sun the Cripple's fame resounded throughout the world and his theories of military strategy were handed down from age to age.

Wu Qi

WU QI, a man from the state of Wey, had a strong *penchant* for the games of warfare. At one time, though, he had even been a student under Master Zeng, an immediate disciple of Confucius, and took service with the Lord of Lu. When the forces of Qi were attacking Lu, the Lord of Lu wished to put Wu Qi in command of his armies, but Wu Qi had taken a woman of Qi as his wife, so the ruler mistrusted him. In order to prove his loyalty to the Lu cause and establish a reputation for himself, Wu Qi killed his wife. He was eventually made commander, led the armies against Qi, and routed the enemy in the field. But in Lu there were people who deliberately and with malicious intent spread certain unsavoury stories about him.

'This Wu Qi is a sly, ruthless fellow,' they said. 'In his youth his family had amassed a considerable fortune in gold. All of it he spent on furthering his vain ambition to become a political client in the service of the various noble lords. But his efforts led to the financial ruin of his family, and when neighbours and relatives were rash enough to ridicule him, he murdered more than thirty of these traducers, fled out through the gate of the Wey capital, and made his way eastwards. All he did when he took leave of his mother was bite his arm and swear he would never return to Wey except as a great minister of state. It was after this that he spent some time as a student under Master Zeng. He had not been with him for very long when his mother died. Since he never even went home to observe the funeral rites, Master Zeng despised him and would have nothing more to do with him. So Wu Qi came to Lu, and here he studied military science and took up service with the Lord of Lu. When the Lord of Lu became suspicious of him, he killed his wife to gain his position as commander. If a small country like ours acquires some reputation through a modicum of military success, then it will attract the ill-willed designs of other mightier princes. Since Lu and Wey are fraternal states, His Majesty's employment of the outlawed Wu Qi represents a rebuff to our friends in Wey.' All this renewed the Lord of Lu's suspicions of Wu Qi, and he relieved him of his post.

Later, when Wu Qi got to know that Margrave Civilitas of Wei [445 – 396] was a ruler with a bright political outlook, he thought of entering his service.

'What sort of person is this Wu Qi?' the Margrave asked his minister Li Ke.

'Well, he's a power-crazed sex-maniac, but his military nous is in a class by itself – not even Grand Marshall Tian Rangju could outmatch him,' was Li Ke's reply.

Acting upon this advice, Margrave Civilitas put Wu Qi in command of his forces. In the attack on the Kingdom of Qin five walled cities fell into his hands.

As a general Wu Qi made a point of eating the same rations and wearing the same clothes as the lowest of his soldiery. At nights he used no bedding, but slept on the ground. When on the march, he had no use for horse or chariot and shouldered his own meagre rations in a common soldier's knapsack, sharing the hardships of his men. Once, when one of his soldiers was afflicted with a gangrenous wound, Wu Qi in person sucked out the pus. On hearing the news of this, the soldier's mother burst into tears.

'Your son is just an ordinary other-rank, yet the general personally sucked out the poison from his wound so what on earth are you crying at?' someone asked her.

'Ah, you just don't understand,' replied the mother. 'Some years back His Excellency Wu Qi sucked out the poison from a wound suffered by the boy's own father, with the result that when my husband went into action he would never show his back to the enemy and died fighting. Now that His Excellency has done the same for the son, there's no saying how soon my boy may meet his death in some battle. That's why I'm weeping.'

Because Wu Qi was an expert operational commander whose frugality, justice, and limitless self-exertion completely captured the loyalty of his men, Margrave Civilitas appointed him Military Governor of the West River Region to guard the frontier against Qin and Hân.

After the death of Margrave Civilitas, Wu Qi continued to serve under his son Margrave Militas [395 – 368]. Once, while sailing through the West River Region together with Wu Qi, Margrave Militas turned and said to him as the boat was travelling in mid-stream, 'What splendidly rugged mountains and what a mighty river. This is the treasure of our nation.'

'It's moral fibre that counts – not natural defences,' objected Wu Qi. 'In olden times, when the Three Miao Tribe held territory flanked by Lakes Dongting and Pengli, they neglected the cultivation of their moral fibre and self-discipline and were destroyed by the Great Yu [(?)2205 – 2198]. King Murderer [(?)1818 – 1766], the last king of the Xia Dynasty, ruled over territory guarded by the Yellow River and River Ji to the west, Mounts Tai and Hua to the east, the Gates of Yi to the south, and Sheep Gut Pass to the north, yet because of his tyranny King Deliverer [1766 – 1754] was able to expel him. King Debauchery [1154 – 1123], the last monarch of the Shang Dynasty, ruled a land bounded by Elder Bastard Gate to its west, the Taihang range to its east, Mount Constancy to its north, and the Great River running along its southern confines, yet because of his decadent government and its effect on morale, King Warrior [1120 – 1122] was able to slay him. Such examples prove beyond any doubt that what counts is moral fibre, not natural defences. If you do not pay attention to good government, these men here in this very boat will all work for your enemies.'

'So very true!' said Margrave Militas and lost no time in confirming Wu Qi's military governorship of the West River Region. All this greatly increased Wu Qi's reputation.

When the State of Wei instituted the office of Prime Minister, Shang Wen was appointed. This displeased Wu Qi. 'May I have a word with you on the subject of merit and achievement in government service?' he asked the new Premier.

Shang Wen consented.

'When it comes to leading armies and inspiring our men with such death-defying courage that enemy states dare not plot against us, which of us comes out best, you or I?' asked Wu Qi.

'You do,' said Shang Wen.

'In controlling the administration, maintaining good relations with the ordinary people, and keeping the treasury and granaries of the nation well stocked, which of us has achieved more, you or I?'

'You have done more than I,' replied Shang Wen.

'And who contributes more towards the defence of the West River region, thus checking the eastward incursions of the Kingdom of Qin and encouraging the submission of Hân and Zhao?'

Once again Shang Wen freely admitted that Wu Qi had made the greater contribution.

'Why is it, then,' asked Wu Qi, 'that, although in all three respects your role has been less than mine, you have been promoted to a higher rank than me?'

'At this particular juncture, with a ruler as tender in years as ours, the body politic is by no means securely established. We are not yet assured of the confidence of the ministers nor do we have the entire trust of the common people. At such a moment, should the onus of responsibility rest upon my shoulders or yours?' asked Shang Wen.

Wu Qi fell silent, and it was some while before he replied, 'Perhaps you would be more suited to the task.'

'That's why,' said Shang Wen, 'I for the present enjoy higher rank than you.'

This interview served to convince Wu Qi that he was not Shang Wen's equal.

On the death of Shang Wen, Gong Shu became Premier. He married the daughter of the Margrave of Wei, and sought to damage the interests of Wu Qi. One of his servants advised him that Wu Qi could easily be removed. Gong Shu asked him how it could be done.

'This Wu Qi,' explained the servant, 'is a stickler for etiquette and propriety and full of his own reputation. You must first go to Margrave Militas and say, "Wu Qi is such a talented man, and your state, Margrave, so small and weak, bordering as it does on the mighty Kingdom of Qin, that in my own humble opinion I doubt very much whether he'll be in a mind to stay here very much longer." Then Margrave Militas will at once ask you what to do, and you should make the following proposition; "Why not offer him one of your daughters in marriage, Your Highness? If he intends to stay, he's bound to accept. If not, then he will refuse. That's the way to find out how things stand with him." When this has been done, you should invite Wu Qi home with you, where you will arrange for your wife the Princess to put on a show of temper and disrespect towards you. When he sees the contemptuous behaviour of one princess to her lord and master, he is bound to refuse the other.'

Just as the servant predicted, when Wu Qi saw what a virago the princess was to her husband the Premier of Wei, he did indeed decline the Margrave's offer. This deprived him of his ruler's trust and confidence; and, fearing recriminations, he left forthwith for the Kingdom of Chu.

For some time King Compassion of Chu [401 – 381] had been aware of Wu Qi's ability, and on his arrival he made him Premier. In this office Wu Qi made himself responsible for the clarification and rigorous enforcement of the laws and the penal code. He dismissed superflous functionaries and remote relatives of the royal house and instead promoted the interests of active military officers. In putting the emphasis on national defence he overrode those politicians who with specious oratory had tried to champion the Twin Alliance System against Qin as a panacea for national salvation. In this way he pacified the barbarian nations of the far south; he annexed the territories of Chen and Cai, and pushed back the incursions of Hân, Wei, and Zhao in the north: and in the west he sent an expedition against the Kingdom of Qin.

The rulers of the other states which had suffered from the new-found might of Chu, and the disposessed aristocracy of Chu itself all desired the ruination of Wu Qi. On the demise of King Compassion of Chu the ministers of the ruling clan ran riot and attacked Wu Qi, who fled to where the King's corpse was lying in state and hid behind it in the hope of saving himself. So eager were his assailants that they actually shot their arrows into the King's corpse as well as at Wu Qi.

After the burial of the King, the Crown Prince succeeded to the throne and had his Chief Minister execute all those who had shot at Wu Qi and the late King's corpse. More than seventy of those found guilty of shooting Wu Qi were annihilated along with their clans.

Historical Commentary

Here follows the Grand Historian's Commentary:

When discussing warfare, many people refer to the Thirteen Treatises on War, *by Master Sun, and* The Rules of War, *by Wu Qi. These are so widely available that further comment by me on the theoretical aspect of their achievements would be superfluous. I shall confine my remarks to the way in which they revealed themselves by their actual deeds.*

'The able may not be eloquent, the eloquent may not be able,' runs a popular adage. Master Sun revealed his brilliance by the manner in which he outwitted Pang Juan, yet earlier on he had insufficient foresight to avoid punishment by mutilation. Wu Qi descanted on the superiority of national morale over natural defences, but when he was in a position to put his theories into practice in the Kingdom of Chu, his harsh repressive measures and his lack of human sympathy cost him his life. Ah, the sadness of it all!

WAR-LORDS

Lord Mengchang

THE LORD OF MENGCHANG'S personal name was Wen and he was a member of the Tian clan. His father was Tian Ying, Lord Pacifier of Guo. This Tian Ying was the younger son of King Awesome of Qi [356 – 319] and was also the younger half-brother of Awesome's successor, King All-Embracing [318 – 301]. Tian Ying held government office from the time of King Awesome onwards, and, along with Zou Ji, Margrave of Cheng, and Tian Ji, he commanded the Qi forces in the campaign against Wei to relieve Hân. Margrave Cheng and Tian Ji vied with each other for royal favour, and the Margrave used underhand methods to damage Tian Ji's reputation and further his own interests. In sheer panic Tian Ji turned against his own nation and attacked the border marches of Qi. His attempt failed, and he fled abroad. On King Awesome's demise King All-Embracing ascended the throne. Being well aware of Margrave Cheng's machinations against Tian Ji, he recalled Tian Ji from exile and appointed him commander. In the second year of his reign Tian Ji, together with Tian Ying and Sun the Cripple, attacked Wei, whose armies they defeated at Horse Mound, capturing Crown Prince Shen of Wei and slaying the Wei commander, Pang Juan. In the seventh year of All-Embracing's reign, Tian Ying went as an envoy to the states of Hân and Wei, which duly recognised Qi's suzerainty. It was Tian Ying who brought about a meeting between the rulers Margrave Resplendent of Hân, King Benevolence of Wei [369 – 318], and King All-Embracing at a place south of Eastern Barrow in the land of Qi. Before parting they concluded a treaty. In the following year there was another conference with King Benevolence at Zhen. That was the year in which Benevolence died.

In the ninth year of King All-Embracing's reign, Tian Ying became Prime Minister of Qi, and it was he who advised the King during his conference at Slow Land with the successor of King Benevolence, King Achiever of Wei [317 – 296]. When the news of Tian Ying's part in this conference reached the ears of the King of Chu, another monarch called Awesome [339 – 329], he was filled with fury towards him. In the following year, Chu attacked and defeated the Qi armies at Slow Land, and some men of Chu were specially detached to pursue Tian Ying in person. Tian Ying induced a certain Zhang Chou to put in a good word for him with Awesome of Chu, and as a result the pursuit was called off. When Tian Ying had been Premier for eleven years King All-Embracing died. King Mercy [300 – 284] succeeded to the throne. Three years later he enfeoffed Tian Ying with the lands of Marshgrass.

Tian Ying had already had forty or more children when one of his lesser concubines gave him a son called Wen – 'the Refined.' This son was born on the fifth day of the fifth month and in consequence Ying superstitiously ordered the mother not to feed him any more. None the less she secretly kept him alive and brought him up. When he was older she used the good offices of his other brothers to introduce Wen into the presence of his father.

'I thought I told you to get rid of that boy,' roared Tian Ying in fury to the mother, 'how dare you let him survive?'

'Sir,' said Wen, kowtowing to his father, 'might I ask why it's not done to rear children born on the fifth day of the fifth month?'

'Such children,' said Tian Ying, 'become so big-headed when they grow up, they can't get through the door, and they bring nothing but trouble to their parents.'

'Might I ask,' inquired Wen, 'is a man's life decreed by fate or by the size of doors?'

For a while Tian Ying was lost for words.

'If it depends on fate,' said Wen, 'then there's no point in worrying yourself over such things. Whereas, if it depends on the door, all you need to do is raise the height of the doorway so that nobody will be too tall to get through.'

'You've already said quite enough for one day,' said Tian Ying.

A considerable while afterwards Wen took another opportunity to put a question to his father.

'What's the son of a son?' he asked.
'A grandson,' the father replied.
'What is the grandson of a grandson?'
'A great-great-grandson.'
'And what is the grandson of a great-great- grandson?'
'I haven't the slightest idea,' said his father.

'All this time you have held office as Prime Minister of Qi under three successive kings,' said Wen, 'and, though the territory of Qi has not been enlarged, your own private fortune has risen to ten thousand pieces of gold. In your whole household you haven't produced a single notable character of worth. I've heard that families of generals must go on producing generals and families of premiers should go on turning out new premiers. The womenfolk in your seraglio tread fine silk, while your gentlemen retainers can't even afford jackets of sackcloth. And again, your slave girls and concubines have a surfeit of choice fare, while your gentlemen go short of even chaff and husks. Now that you've amassed such an enormous fortune, do you mean to tell me that you intend to bequeath it to people of whom you haven't the slightest idea, and also to remain impervious to the fact that affairs of state are daily going to rack and ruin? Your attitude, if you'll pardon my saying it, simply amazes me.'

From then on Tian Ying treated his son Wen with the greatest courtesy, putting him in charge of his household with the special care of his clients and retainers. Daily more clients offered their services, until Wen's reputation resounded through all the allied states and their princes sent envoys to Tian Ying, Master of Marshgrass, with the suggestion that he appoint Wen his heir and successor. He agreed to this. On his death he was awarded the posthumous title of Lord Pacifier of Guo, and Wen duly took his place as Master of Marshgrass, later to be known as Lord Mengchang.

Once Master of Marshgrass, Lord Mengchang welcomed retainers and clients from all the other states, and even criminals on the run found refuge in his household. In his generous treatment of retainers he gave liberally of his inheritance. In this way he acquired a monopoly of the world's talented men. Among all the thousands of clients in his household he made no distinction of high or low, but placed all on a par with himself.

When he sat in converse with any of his clients, he would always have a scribe behind the screen whose task it was to record the conversation. During such conversations he would inquire after the addresses of the client's close relatives. As soon as the man left his presence, he would send someone round to convey his kindest regards to the relatives and shower them with presents.

On one occasion, while he was entertaining his retainers to a late-night feast, he noticed one of them sulking in the shadows away from the torchlight. The man supposed his food to be inferior to that of the others and in his anger stopped eating and took his leave. Lord Mengchang rose and personally carried out his own food to show him that it was the same as everyone else's. Unbearably ashamed, the client cut his own throat. This incident brought even more fine gentlemen into Lord Mengchang's service. So uniformly considerate was his excellent treatment of all his retainers that every one of them thought himself the recipient of special favour.

King Resplendent of Qin [306 – 251] heard of Mengchang's outstanding qualities and sent Lord Jingyang as a hostage and token of his good faith to Qi in return for an audience in Qin with Lord Mengchang. Though Mengchang was prepared to go to Qin, all his retainers were opposed to the journey. All the same, he ignored their advice and insisted he should go.

'On my way here this morning,' said the rhetorician Su Dai, 'I met two toy men, one of wood and one of clay. They were having a chat. "You'll have had your lot if it rains," said the wooden one.

' "I was born of clay, and when my time comes, to clay I shall return," said the other. "But if it does rain now, you will be washed clean away, and who knows where you'll end up?"

'Now Qin is a regular den of wolves and tigers, yet you're thinking of making a trip there. Should anything stop you coming back, you'll really be giving the clay man something to laugh about, won't you?'

This was enough to make Mengchang cancel his journey.

In the twenty-fifth year of the reign of King Mercy of Qi the King of Qin finally succeeded in inveigling Lord Mengchang into Qin. On his arrival King Resplendent at once made him Premier of the nation.

'Lord Mengchang is a man of considerable ability,' said someone to the King of Qin, 'but he also happens to be a native of Qi. Now that he is Premier, he's bound to put Qi's interests before those of Qin. It's a dangerous situation for us here in Qin.'

This remark changed the King's attitude. He had Mengchang confined until he could find a suitable occasion to do away with him. Lord Mengchang managed to send a messenger to the King's most favoured concubine entreating her to seek his release.

'My lord,' the favourite asked Mengchang, 'wouldn't it be nice if I could have a silver-fox coat like yours to wear?'

Now, although Mengchang had owned a silver-fox fur coat worth a thousand pieces of gold and unmatched throughout the world, he had already presented it to the King of Qin on his arrival and had no other fur coat with him. In extreme perplexity, he sought advice from all his followers, but not one of them had any suggestion to offer, until from the back of the gathering a certain accomplished cat-burglar spoke up.

'I'm your man. I'll get back your fur coat.'

That very night, as sly as an alley cat, he slipped into the treasure-vault of the Qin palace, purloined the coat, and presented it to the King's favourite. In return she put in a word for Mengchang with the King, who presently released him.

Once out of confinement, Lord Mengchang took off as quickly as possible, altering the particulars of identity in his passport so that he could get past the frontier police. In the middle of the same night he reached Box Valley Pass.

Meanwhile King Resplendent had been having second thoughts about releasing Lord Mengchang. He sent someone to summon him, but discovered he had already made his get-away. At once he sent relays of horsemen in pursuit.

Now, Lord Mengchang was already at the pass, but since the regulations stipulated that people were only allowed past the frontier barrier at cock-crow, he was fearful that his pursuers would catch up with him. Among the more obscure members of his retinue there happened to be one who was very good at farmyard impersonations and could imitate cocks crowing. No sooner had this client done his party piece than all the cockerels far and near started to crow in unison. At this the fugitives' passports were promptly examined and they were allowed through. In the time that it takes to eat a snack, the Qin pursuers arrived at the pass, only to discover that Lord Mengchang's band had already left the country. They abandoned pursuit and went back.

Previously, when Lord Mengchang had ranked the cat-burglar and farmyard impersonator among his retainers, all the others had felt it an insult to their own dignity. But in the end, when real trouble cropped up in Qin, it transpired that only these two were able to extricate him. Thereafter the other clients held the cat-burglar and the impersonator in great esteem.

While Lord Mengchang was passing through the State of Zhao, Lord Flat Plain of Zhao entertained him. Having heard of Mengchang's great reputation, the people of Zhao flocked into the streets to take a look at him.

'Just fancy,' they said roaring with laughter, 'we used to think the Master of Marshgrass was really something great, but now we can see what a pathetic little fellow he really is.'

LORD MENGCHANG

When such talk came to his ears, Lord Mengchang fell into a rage, and his retainers and other henchmen waded into the crowd hacking and chopping, and cut down several hundred people. Then they proceeded to lay waste the whole country before departing.

King Mercy of Qi felt ill at ease for having sent Mengchang off to Qin: so, when Lord Mengchang returned, he put him at the head of his government. Such was Mengchang's resentment towards Qin that, though at first he was going to revive an old alliance with Hân and Wei to attack Chu, instead he joined forces with those two states to launch a campaign against Qin. It was his intention to obtain troops and provender from the region of West Zhou. Su Dai spoke up for West Zhou.

'My lord,' he said, 'for nine years you served Hân's and Wei's interests by using Qi to fight their wars against Chu, and you wrested from Chu the regions of Hummock and Sheh and areas to their north. These went to bolster up the power of Hân and Wei. By now attacking Qin you will be adding further to the strength of Hân and Wei. If they are relieved of worries about Chu to their south and Qin to their west, then things will be dangerous for your own Kingdom of Qi. Hân and Wei are bound to lose respect for Qi, as they overawe Qin. And this, I would think, will put you in a dangerous situation, my lord. Wouldn't it be best for you to arrange for us here in West Zhou to do all we can to get on good terms with Qin? Desist from attacking Qin, and give up your idea of levying troops and provender from our region. You should menace the gates of Qin at Box Valley Pass, but make no move to attack. Instead you will use our good offices to convey a message to King Resplendent of Qin along these lines; "The Master of Marshgrass has no intention of strengthening Hân and Wei by conquering Qin. If he attacks you, it will only be in his desire to bring pressure upon you to make the King of Chu cede the Eastern Lands to Qi and for you to restore peace by releasing King Cherisher of Chu." If you will allow us to come to favourable terms with Qin in this matter, Qin, to avoid being conquered, is bound to be willing to cede the Eastern Lands in exchange. The King of Chu will obtain his release and will consequently be bound to consider Qi his benefactor. Qi, in turn, will be strengthened by the acquisition of the Eastern Lands; and your own demesne of Marshgrass can rest free from anxiety for ages to come. As long as Qin is not excessively weakened and still menaces Hân, Wei, and Zhao from the west, these three states are certain to look up to Qi as their protector.'

'Excellent advice,' said the Master of Marshgrass. Accordingly he encouraged Hân and Wei to go out of their way to make friendly overtures to Qin and restrained the three states of Hân, Wei, and Zhao from any further campaign. Nor did he levy troops or provender from West Zhou. At this time King Cherisher of Chu [328 – 299] was being held captive in Qin; and, although the state of Qi insisted on his release, Qin to the end refused to keep the bargain and would not let him go.

In his period as Chancellor Lord Mengchang employed a bailiff called Master Wei, who made three trips to collect the revenues from his estates, but never once brought back anything to show for his pains. Lord Mengchang tackled him about it.

'My lord,' said Master Wei, 'I came across a splendid fellow and took it upon myself to make him a loan. That's why I haven't brought anything back with me.'....

Lord Menchang was furious and dismissed him from his service.

Several years passed, and someone slandered Mengchang to King Mercy of Qi, pretending that he was planning to rebel. As a result, when Tian Ji menaced King Mercy, the King suspected Lord Mengchang of having been behind the incident. Menchang took refuge in flight. The gentleman who had been given the loan of grain by Master Wei heard of this matter and petitioned the King in a letter which explained that Mengchang was not the sort of man to rebel. He declared that he would vouch for him with his own life. Then he cut his own throat at the palace gate to try and restore Mengchang's unsullied reputation. King Mercy was astounded by this, and made a thorough investigation about the matter which proved indeed that Mengchang had not been party to any plot of rebellion. So he recalled him to court. Warned by his recent experience, Lord Mengchang pleaded illness, and asked if he might pass his old age on his estates at Marshgrass. King Mercy consented.

Later on, General Lü Li, a refugee from Qin, was appointed Chancellor of Qi. He tried to cause trouble for the rhetorician Su Dai, so Dai spoke to Lord Mengchang.

'Zhou Zou, you remember,' he said, 'was extremely loyal to Qi, yet the King expelled him and listened to the advice of Qin Fu. Now Chancellor Lü Li wishes to establish friendly relations with the Kingdom of Qin. If Qi and Qin become allies, then Qin Fu and Lü Li will both become dominant. If they both occupy positions of power in Qi, then consider yourself of no account! Your best policy would be to hasten north with troops to bring pressure on Zhao to make its peace with Qin and Wei and then to bring back Zhou Zou and restore him to the King of Qi's confidence by praising his loyalty. In doing so you will at the same time have averted a calamitous change in the balance of power. If Qi is not in league with Qin, then all the other States will acknowledge the leadership of Qi. Qin Fu, fallen from grace, will undoubtedly flee the country. Then to whom do you think the King of Qi will entrust the government of his state?'

Lord Mengchang proceeded upon this plan, inevitably incurring the resentment of Lü Li, who schemed to do him a mischief. Fearful for his life, Mengchang sent a letter to the Premier of Qin, Wei Ran, Margrave of Rang.

'I have heard that Qin wants to use Lü Li to bring about an alliance with Qi,' the letter went, 'Qi is the most powerful state in the world. Should this alliance be accomplished, your prestige will suffer a severe blow. If Qi and Qin become confederates to menace Hân, Wei, and

Zhao, it will be Lü Li who will become Chancellor of both, mark my words. To put it another way, not only will you be furthering the fortunes of Qi, but you will also be consolidating your enemy Lü Li's position. If Qi is enabled to keep out of such world-wide military action, Lü Li will certainly bear you a very deep grudge. Your best course is to persuade the King of Qin to attack Qi, for if Qi is defeated, I would like, if I may, to enfeoff you with my own gains. Once Qi is defeated, Qin will be apprehensive about the strength of Hân, Wei, and Zhao, and will consider you a key man for the furtherance of good relations with these three nations. Hân, Wei and Zhao are inferior in power to Qi, and will fear the might of Qin. Thus they, too, will look up to you as the man to secure them the good-will of Qin. In this way Qi, in defeat, will consider that you have rendered her a service, while Hân, Wei, and Zhao, pincered between powerful states, will look up to you as a diplomatic mediator. And thus your fief in Qi will be assured, whilst Qin and the three states of Hân, Wei, and Zhao will make much of you for having secured friendly diplomatic relations for them. If, on the other hand Qi is not defeated, and Lü Li is restored to favour and power in Qin, you will be done for.'

When he read this letter, Margrave Rang advised King Resplendent of Qin to attack Qi, and Lü Li fled the country.

Later, when King Mercy of Qi conquered Song, he became more arrogant than ever and wanted to be rid of Lord Mengchang. In fear for his life Lord Mengchang moved to the state of Wei, where King Resplendent of Wei [295 – 277] made him his Chancellor. Then he made an alliance with Qin in the west. Zhao and Yan made a combined attack upon Qi, whose armies they routed. King Mercy fled and came to rest at Ju, where he shortly afterwards died. King Achiever [283 – 265] succeeded him on the throne of Qi. Lord Mengchang now stood in a neutral position towards all the other princes of the world, with allegiance to none. Having newly come to the throne, King Achiever was apprehensive about Mengchang, so he made overtures to him and secured his goodwill by reinstating him as Master of Marshgrass. Lord Mengchang was in fact the posthumous title of Tian Wen, Master of Marshgrass. His many sons disputed the succession to his estates, and both Qi and Wei combined to wipe out the demense of Marshgrass. His line came to an end, and no descendants of his survive in the present age.

An earlier incident in the life of Mengchang involves Feng Huan, who had heard that Lord Mengchang was keen on gathering together clients and retainers, and went for an interview with him, for which he turned up in shabby straw sandals.

'Venerable sir,' said Lord Mengchang, 'you've humbled yourself to come so far to see me; what learned counsels have you to offer me?'

'Well, my lord,' said Feng, 'I've just heard that you are fond of the company of fine men, and being hard up myself I've come along to offer my services.'

Lord Mengchang installed him for the first ten days in the Transit Quarters, after which he asked the warden of the Transit Quarters how the new guest was shaping up.

'A real down-and-out, that Master Feng,' said the warden. 'All he's got is one sword, and even the hilt-binding of that is made from plaited straw. He has this habit of flexing the sword blade and singing a little ditty:

> '*Long sword, long sword,*
> *back home we'll steal;*
> *we get no fish*
> *to pep up our meal.*'

Mengchang promptly transferred Feng to the Welcome Visitors' Quarters, where fish was included in his meals.

Five days later Mengchang again spoke to the warden.

'He's been flexing that sword and singing again,' the warden replied. 'This time he sings:

> *'Long sword, long sword,*
> *O let us go home;*
> *no transport's provided*
> *for us to roam.'*

This time Lord Mengchang transferred him to the Staff Quarters, and wherever Feng went a carriage was put at his disposal. Five days afterwards Mengchang again had a word with the warden.

'It's the same story,' he said, 'but this time he sings:

> *'Long sword, we'd be better off, I fear,*
> *There's nothing vaguely homelike here.'*

This did not please Lord Mengchang.

Feng's year of residence passed without his even offering so much as one single word of counsel or advice. At this time Lord Mengchang was Chancellor of Qi and had been enfeoffed with ten thousand households in Marshgrass. He had three thousand dependent clients, but the income from his estates was not enough for their upkeep. He had authorised his bailiffs to lend money in the form of copper cash to the farmers of Marshgrass, and for more than a year none of the loans had been repaid and most of the debtors would not even pay the interest. Very soon it would be impossible for him to provide for his retainers any further. In his anxiety he felt obliged to turn to his immediate staff and inquire if there was possibly anyone to whom he could entrust the business of debt-collecting.

'There's that client in your Staff Quarters,' said the warden, 'Master Feng, he's got the air, he's got the looks, he's a clever talker, and he's a big fellow. What's more, he's no good for anything else. He's the very man to send on a rent-collecting jaunt.'

LORD MENGCHANG

So Mengchang had Feng Huan ushered into his presence and put his request to him.

'Unaware of my base inadequacies,' he said, 'more than three thousand clients have favoured me with their company. The income from my estates is insufficient to keep my beloved guests at the standard they deserve. With this in mind I laid out money loans to the farmers of Marshgrass by way of investment. But when the harvest came round in Marshgrass, it brought no returns for me. The people there just did not give me the interest due. I'm afraid I shall not be able to keep my honoured guests in food. Might I ask you, venerable sir, to collect these debts?'

'Certainly,' Feng Huan replied, then took his leave, and set off to Marshgrass. There he summoned all those who had borrowed money from Mengchang to a meeting. At this he obtained money and interest to the amount of one hundred thousand cash from them. He spent this on the brewing of a great deal of rice-wine and the purchase of many fattened oxen. Next he summoned all the debtors, telling them all to come along whether or not it lay within their power to repay the debts. All of them were to bring their loan-deeds so that he could check with his records. On the day they were all assembled together he had the oxen slaughtered and the wine brought in for a mighty feast. When the party was in full swing, he checked the records, as previously announced. To those who could afford to repay the debt he allowed a fixed time-limit for settlement; and, in the case of those who could not afford to pay back what they owed, he simply took their loan deeds and burned them.

'The reason,' he said, 'why Lord Mengchang made these loans was that some of you were unable to make your basic living from agriculture. The reason why he's now asking for the interest is simply that he hasn't the wherewithal for the upkeep of his retainers. For the more well-to-do we'll allow some time for repayment. For those who are hard pressed we'll simply burn the loan-deeds and call it a day. And now gentlemen, just get stuck into the food and drink. With a liege lord like the one we've got, you could never let him down, could you?'

All present rose to their feet and gave him a standing ovation.

When Lord Mengchang heard that Feng Haun had burnt the loan deeds, he was furious and sent for him.

'Now, look,' said Mengchang when Feng Huan appeared, 'here I am with three thousand clients dependent on me. It was for their sakes that I made loans to the farmers of Marshgrass. My estates are small, and to make matters worse most of the people don't repay their loans on time. It was because I feared my clients might go short of food that I asked you, sir, to collect the debts. Now I've heard that when you got your hands on some of the money, you straight away used most of it on oxen and wine for a party. Then you went and burned the loan deeds. Might I trouble you for an explanation, sir?'

'Yes, that's quite right,' said Feng Huan. 'If I hadn't laid out a great deal on food, meat, and wine for the party, I wouldn't have been able to get them all together for a meeting. Nor would I have had any means of finding out who could afford to pay up and who couldn't. Those who could I allowed a time-limit in which to pay. As for those who couldn't afford to pay at all, even if we'd kept their loan-deeds and pestered them for ten years, with the interest building up all the time, they would be bound sooner or later to get into a panic and take to flight – thus cancelling the debt off their own bat. In such circumstances we'd still have had nothing by way of return. Going about things like that you would acquire the nasty reputation of being a grasping, avaricious overlord lacking in any affection for your gentry and people, while in turn it would give them the ill-odour of being a people disaffected from their overlord who renegue on their debts. That's no way either to bring out the finer qualities of your people or to increase the lustre of your own fame. All I did was burn useless deeds for an irredeemable loan and wind up some accounts that could never be settled. By doing so I have secured you the love of the people of Marshgrass and boosted your good name. What are you beefing about?' Lord Mengchang clapped his hands with delight and thanked Feng Huan.

LORD MENGCHANG

Slanders emanating from the Kingdom of Qin and Chu led the King of Qi astray by putting it about that Lord Mengchang enjoyed greater prestige than his sovereign and was wielding the real power in Qi. As a result of such rumours the King dismissed Mengchang, and when his retainers and clients learned of his dismissal, they all deserted him.

'My lord,' said Feng Huan, 'lend me a chariot to take me into Qin, and I can promise you that it will do your reputation a power of good and add further to your estates. What do you say to it?'

Lord Mengchang ordered him a chariot for the journey and a sum of money to cover his expenses, then sent him on his way. Feng Huan travelled westwards and tried to present political policies to the King of Qin.

'Itinerant policy-mongers from all ends of the world come dashing full-pelt in their chariots to Qin here in the west,' said Feng Huan, 'and every single one of them is bent on strengthening Qin at the expense of Qi. While those who dash off to Qi in the east are determined to further the interests of Qi and weaken Qin. One of these two nations will be the cock and the other the hen of this world. In the situation as it is, it is impossible to have two cockerels co-existing. The nation that emerges cock of the roost will rule the world.'

The King of Qin prostrated himself in his eagerness to learn Feng Huan's advice.

'Could you suggest any way,' he asked, 'whereby Qin might avoid ending up as the hen bird?'

'Your Majesty,' replied Feng Huan, 'is no doubt aware that the King of Qi has dismissed Lord Mengchang?'

'So I am informed,' said the King of Qin.

'It was Lord Mengchang,' said Feng Huan, 'who made Qi the most powerful nation in the world. Now that the King of Qi has dismissed him on the basis of certain slanders, Mengchang is filled with deep resentment and can be counted on to turn his back on Qi. If he does so, and comes over to Qin, then all his affection for Qi and his devoted service will be transferred to Qin. This will enable you to take over the territory of Qi itself. Then indeed your position as cockerel will be assured beyond any doubt. You should quickly send envoys with money to welcome Lord Mengchang into your camp, for this is an opportunity not to be missed. Should the King of Qi come to his senses and reinstate Mengchang, then it will be impossible to predict who will be cock and who will be hen.'

Delighted with this advice, the King of Qin despatched ten chariots with two thousand taels of gold to buy the allegiance of Lord Mengchang. Feng Huan took his leave and set off in advance of the chariot train. When he arrived at Qi, he offered policies and advice to the King of Qi.

'Itinerant policy-mongers from all ends of the world come dashing full-pelt in their chariots to Qi here in the east,' said Feng Huan, 'and every single one of them is bent on strengthening Qi at the expense of Qin. While those who dash off to Qin in the west are determined to further the interests of Qin and weaken Qi. So one of these two nations will be the cock and the other the hen. If Qin grows powerful, then perforce Qi must be weak. Now, it has recently come to my ears that Qin is sending envoys with ten chariots loaded with two thousand taels of gold to try and buy the services of Lord Mengchang. If he refuses to go westwards to Qin, all well and good. But if he does, and becomes Prime Minister of Qin, then the whole world will go over to their side. Qin will be the rooster and Qi very much the hen, and even our capitals Blackbank and Inkside will be imperilled. Why don't you steal a march on the Qin envoys before they arrive by restoring Lord Mengchang to power and augmenting his fiefs in apology? He is bound to be heartened by your gesture and accept your offer and apology. However powerful the state of Qin may be, it has no right to try to win over the premiers of other nations. You will have confounded the Qin machinations and cut short their bid to wrest the hegemony of the world.'

'Excellent advice,' said the King, and sent spies to the frontier to await the arrival of the Qin envoys. As soon as the envoys crossed the frontiers of Qi, these spies galloped back post-haste to inform the King. He at once summoned Lord Mengchang and reinstated him as Premier, at the same time granting him his old fief, and adding a thousand

LORD MENGCHANG

households to it. When the envoys from Qin heard that Mengchang had been made Chancellor again, they turned their chariots round and departed.

Now, at the time when Mengchang had been dismissed by the King of Qi through the mischief slanders had done to his reputation, all his clients had deserted him. No sooner was he restored to favour than he summoned them back to reinstate them in his household. Feng Huan was charged with the task of welcoming them back. Just before they were due to arrive, Lord Mengchang heaved a great sigh.

'I've always been well inclined towards clients,' he said, 'always tried never to put a foot wrong in my dealings with them all. As you well know, venerable sir, I used to support over three thousand followers in my service. But the moment they knew I was dismissed they turned their backs and deserted me to a man. None of them spared me a single thought. Now that, thanks only to you, sir, I have regained my former office, how can they dare show their faces here again? If they have the cheek to turn up, make no mistake about it, I'll spit in their eyes and heap insult after insult upon them.'

At these remarks Feng Huan tied up the reins and got out of his chariot to bow down before his lord. Mengchang alighted from the chariot and helped him to his feet.

'Venerable sir,' he asked, 'are you making apologies on behalf of the other clients?'

'I'm not apologising for the clients,' said Feng, 'I'm just expressing my concern at hearing you say something so utterly inappropriate. "In all matter there is an intrinsic inevitability. In all events there is embodied a predetermination." Surely, you understand what that means, don't you?'

'Stupid of me,' replied Mengchang, 'but I'm not quite sure what you're driving at.'

'Death comes to all things – such is the intrinsic inevitability of matter. To be rich and enjoy high rank and office and to have the allegiance of numerous fine gentlemen, then to be poor and lowly and lack friends and companions, such circumstances follow a predetermined course. Have you ever noticed, my lord, how people rush to market in the morning, at first light elbowing and shoving their way through the city gates? By the time dusk sets in, those who pass by the lines of market stalls slouch along indifferently without so much as a glance at anything around them. It is not that they love the morning and hate the evening, it is simply that by that hour nothing they had set their hearts on is any longer to be found in the market. Now, in your case, you lost your office, so your clients simply left you. That's no reason to bear those gentlemen a grudge and for no good cause to abandon the practice of keeping clients and retainers. What I'd prefer you to do when you meet your former clients is treat them just as you did in the old days.'

Again and again Lord Mengchang bowed to Feng Huan.

'My dear sir,' he said, 'I shall do exactly as you instruct me. Your words have taught me a lesson which I shall certainly take to heart.'

Historical Commentary

Here follows the Grand Historian's commentary:

I once passed through the Marshgrass region. It is common in the villages and small towns there to encounter whole gangs of violent young fellows. In this respect it is quite different from the neighbouring regions of Zou and Lu. I enquired about the reason behind the violence prevalent in the area. Lord Mengchang, I was told, brought wandering swashbucklers and villains from all over the world flocking into Marshgrass till they and their dependents numbered more than sixty thousand. Historical records tell us that Lord Mengchang delighted in the pastime of collecting clients. A reputation well earned, I would suggest!

Lord Flat Plain

LORD FLAT PLAIN was Zhao Sheng, one of the princes of the royal house of Zhao, of whom he was the most outstanding. His keen patronage of talented men had attracted to his household several thousand followers and retainers. He served as Prime Minister first to King Benevolent Civility of Zhao [298 – 266], then to King Perfect Filiality of Zhao [265 – 245]. Three times he was removed from office and three times he was reinstated. In the end he was given the fief attached to East War citadel.

Lord Flat Plain's manor commanded a view over the houses of his people. In one of their homes lived a cripple: and one day he was hobbling out to fetch water, when a beautiful concubine dwelling in the Lord's manor looked down from her chamber and burst out into mocking laughter at the sight of him. The following day the cripple presented himself at the manor with a strange request.

'I have heard,' he said, 'that you, my lord, delight in the company of true gentlemen. Some of them feel it is not too far to come a thousand miles to join you, simply because you have even more respect for honourable men than love for concubines. It is my misfortune to have a crippling deformity. This attracted the scornful laughter of one of your palace ladies. I beg you, therefore, to give me her head.'

Lord Flat Plain laughingly assented to this request. But as soon as the cripple was out of the way, the lord turned in jest to those around him.

'Did you hear that ridiculous specimen?' he said, 'For the sake of one laugh he'd have me kill my beauty. Isn't that just asking a little too much?'

In spite of his promise, he had no intention of killing the girl, but after a year or so he was amazed to find that one by one more than half of his followers had withdrawn from his service.

'In my treatment of you gentlemen,' he said, 'I have never been discourteous in any way. Why are so many of you leaving my service?'

One of his followers stepped forward to reply.

'When you failed to kill the girl who mocked the cripple, my lord, they assumed that your love of sex was stronger than your respect for men of honour,' he said.

At this Lord Flat Plain had his concubine beheaded and went in person to the house of the cripple to present the head and apologise for his discourtesy. Gradually his retainers started to return to him.

It was just at this time that Lord Mengchang in the State of Qi, Lord Trust Tumulus in the State of Wei, and Lord Chunshen in the Kingdom of Chu, were engaged in competition with one another to attract men of honour and ability.

When the Kingdon of Qin was laying siege to Handan, capital of Zhao, Lord Flat Plain was sent as an emissary to seek aid in the form of an alliance with the Kingdom of Chu. He arranged that he would have twenty retainers accompany him, all of them to be men of courage and powerful physique and skilled in both civil and military accomplishments.

'If our mission can be accomplished by diplomacy alone, so much the better,' he said. 'Failing that, I swear that we shall return only when we have forced them in their own mighty palace hall to agree to an alliance. I shall not seek my knights elsewhere. It will be enough for me to seek them among my own retainers.'

Though he managed to find nineteen men to accompany him, none of his other followers seemed suitable, and, try as he would, he still could not make up the required number. A man called Mao Sui stepped forward from amongst the retainers to recommend himself to his lord.

'I have heard, my lord,' he said, 'that you are trying to make an alliance with Chu and that you are going to choose your companions for this mission from amongst us, your retainers. Now I see you are one man short. Let me make up the quota and travel with you.'

'Sir,' replied Lord Flat Plain, 'for how many years have you been one of my household?'

LORD FLAT PLAIN

'I have been here three years,' said Mao Sui.

'In this world of ours a man of talent is a needle in a sack – he immediately reveals his acuity,' said Lord Flat Plain. 'Now you, my good sir, have been with me some three years, yet so far I have heard not a single word about you from my followers. Not having heard anything about you, my good sir, leads me to assume that there isn't much to you. No, my good sir, you're just not up to it. You, my good sir, will stay put.'

'Why not try putting me in the sack just this once,' replied Mao Sui. 'If you'd done that earlier, you'd have seen all of the needle, not just its point.'

Finally Lord Flat Plain allowed Mao Sui to accompany him. The other nineteen followers cast Mao Sui derisory looks, but did not choose to laugh out loud. Yet by the time they reached the Kingdom of Chu, Mao Sui, after long discussions of policy with them, had won their entire respect and confidence.

Lord Flat Plain and the King of Chu met to hold a conference about the possibility of an alliance against Qin and to discuss its advantages and disadvantages. The talks started at dawn and were still going on at midday without their having reached any decision.

'You're needed up there, good sir,' said the other nineteen to Mao Sui.

With his hand on his sword-hilt he made his way straight up the steps to where his lord was seated.

'The pros and cons of this business can be settled in a couple of words,' he said. 'How come you've been jawing about alliances since sunrise to noon and still nothing's been decided?'

'And just who is this gentleman?' the King of Chu asked Lord Flat Plain.

'He is one of my retainers,' replied the lord.

'Get down there where you came from!' bellowed the King, 'I happen to be talking to your lord, so what the devil are you doing here?'

Still with his hand on his sword-hilt Mao Sui advanced towards the King.

'So,' he countered, 'you feel you can bellow at me because you have the hosts of Chu behind you. But right now there's no more than ten paces between us, so I wouldn't put too much trust in the hosts of Chu. Your life's thread hangs from my fingers. What do you mean by bellowing at me in my lord's presence? I have heard that King Perfect Deliverer [1766 – 1754] ruled the world from thirty square miles of territory, and that from fifty square miles of soil King Civility, [who reigned until 1123], made all the princes of the world his vassals. Do you think they achieved this simply by having vast armies behind them? Certainly not. The fact is, they knew how to manipulate the situation to their own advantage and inspire complete awe by their prestige. Here you are now with three thousand square miles of territory and a million halberdiers at your disposal. That's what I'd call the stuff to make a hegemon! There's nothing in the world to stop a state as strong as Chu. What a miserable specimen that General Bai Qi is that they make so much of in Qin! With his great army of sixty or seventy thousand he did battle with your kingdom. In the first encounter he captured Yen and your capital Ying. In the second he burnt your Royal Tumuli and Mausolea. And with the third battle he humiliated your father. Here indeed is good cause for a hundred years of vengeful hatred. If the State of Zhao senses this shame, how is it that the King of Chu remains insensible to it? This alliance is all for Chu's sake, not for Zhao's. So what do you mean by bellowing at me in my lord's presence?'

'Quite right, sir, quite right,' replied the King of Chu. 'It is just as you say. I shall back this alliance with my country's whole-hearted support.'

'Is the alliance concluded, then?' asked Mao Sui.

'It is,' affirmed the King.

Mao Sui now directed the King's attendants to bring the blood of chickens, dogs, and horses. Kneeling before the King he presented him with a copper bowl full of blood of the sacrificial beasts.

'Drink up, Your Majesty. You next, my lord. Then me, last. That'll conclude our alliance!'

The alliance thus settled in the throne palace itself, Mao Sui grasped the votive bowl in his left hand and beckoned to his companions below.

'You gents down there,' he shouted. 'Quench your thirst with this blood. You've been very busy getting other folks to do the dirty work for you.'

On the conclusion of the alliance Lord Flat Plain returned to Zhao. 'Never again.' he said. 'will I dare set myself up as a judge of able men. I must have selected thousands in my time. I never suspected that one gifted knight would ever slip through my fingers. Now I realise how mistaken I was about you, Master Mao. No sooner had you reached Chu than you sent our nation's fame ringing through the whole world. With no more than your tongue you proved more forceful than an army of a million men. No, never again will I dare set myself up as a connoisseur of ability.'

From then on Mao Sui became his most honoured retainer.

After Lord Flat Plain had returned to Zhao, the King of Chu sent Lord Chunshen at the head of troops to relieve Zhao, whilst Lord Trust Tumulus also seized control of the Jin Frontier Army to come to the rescue of Zhao. Before either arrived, the Qin armies had reached the capital, Handan. The situation in the capital was so critical that there was talk of surrender, much to the distress of Lord Flat Plain. Li Tan, the son of the Warden of the Diplomatic Reception Centre, came to offer his advice.

'Aren't you concerned about the destruction of our nation?' he asked Lord Flat Plain.

'If Zhao goes under,' replied the lord, 'the best we can expect is a life of servitude. Only a fool could fail to be disturbed.'

'Well,' said Li Tan, 'the citizens of Handan have reached the state where they are bartering their children with each other, using the bones for kindling, and eating the flesh. What you might call something of a crisis, don't you think? And there you are with hundreds of women in your seraglio, concubines and slave-girls dressed in brocades and damask, and your kitchen overflowing with cereals and meats, while the average citizen doesn't have even a sackcloth jacket to his back and can't even get enough dregs and chaff to fill his belly. The people are on their last legs, and, with no weapons to go round, some of them are reduced to sharpening sticks to serve as spears and arrows, whilst here's your palace cluttered up with precious bronze musical instruments that could easily be melted down for the war effort. If Qin conquers us, do you think they'll allow you to hang on to them? On the other hand if Zhao manages to survive, you are not likely to go short of such things are you, my lord? Why don't you take it on yourself to enlist everyone in your household from your main wife downwards as officers and soldiers, so that they can play their part, too? Liquidate all your possessions to supply rations to the soldiers. Now that the troops have their backs to the wall, it's an easy time for you to earn yourself a name for magnanimity dirt cheap, at the same time as bucking up their spirits.'

Lord Flat Plain did as he advised, and the country gained three thousand fine warriors, every one of them ready to die for Zhao. With these men Li Tan sallied forth to do battle against Qin and drove the enemy back some thirty miles. Once his storm-troop battalions joined forces with the relief columns from Chu and Wei, the Qin armies lifted the siege and withdrew. Handan was given a new lease of life. Li Tan was killed in action, but his father was enfeoffed as Margrave of Li.

Since it was Lord Flat Plain's doing that had brought Lord Trust Tumulus to the relief of Handan, Yu the Grand Vizier mooted an increase of fief for Flat Plain. Hearing of the Vizier's intention, the great sophist Gongsun Long rode by night straight to Flat Plain's residence.

'Is it true that the Vizier intends to suggest an increase of your fief?' he asked.

Lord Flat Plain admitted that that was the case.

'That just won't do,' said Gongsun Long. 'The reason why His Majesty made you Prime Minister of Zhao was not that your sort of nous was unique in Zhao. Nor was it for any achievements on your part, or any lack of merit on the part of others, that he awarded you the fief of East War citadel. It was simply because you are one of his close relatives. When you were offered the Prime Minister's seal, you failed to point out that you were lacking in qualifications: and when you were offered the fief, you never suggested that you'd done nothing to deserve it. You accepted each as some natural prerogative of a relative. If a further fief is conferred on you now, it will be a case of a relative gaining a city, whilst the meritorious man whose foresight and fine deeds were actually responsible for saving the situation remains unrewarded. It's quite out of the question, I'm afraid. Anyway, Yu the Vizier is sitting pretty whatever happens, for if you obtain your fief, he will be round knocking at your door like a debt-collector! And if the request is turned down, he will have gained the gratuitous reputation of having tried to do you a favour. Whatever you do, don't listen to his suggestion.'

Lord Flat Plain consequently ignored Vizier Yu's proposal.

In the fifteenth year of King Perfect Filiality of Zhao [265 – 245], Lord Flat Plain died. His descendants survived until Zhao itself fell to the armies of the first Emperor of Qin. Lord Flat Plain was a generous patron of Gongsun Long, an outstanding rhetorician noted for his skilful logical disputation *On Hardness and Whiteness*, until one day Zou Yan came to Zhao, discoursed on ultimate truth as opposed to mere captiousness, and by his arguments earned Gongsun Long's instant dismissal.

Yu the Vizier was originally just another itinerant politician. Slouching along in straw sandals with a peasant's thatched umbrella slung nonchalantly over his shoulder, he came touting his policies to none other than King Perfect Filiality himself. At the very first audience he was awarded two thousand taels of gold and a pair of precious discs of white jade. At the next he was made the Grand Vizier of Zhao and from then on was always referred to as Yu the Vizier. When the armies of Zhao were locked in battle during the Long Level campaign against Qin, Zhao failed to carry the field and lost a high-ranking general. The King of Zhao summoned the Commander-in-Chief of the army, Lou Chang, and Yu the Grand Vizier.

'We've failed to secure victory and have lost a general into the bargain,' said the King. 'What do you say to my donning armour and leading my forces in person against the enemy?'

'That would be of no help,' said Commander Lou Chang. 'Better to send a high-ranking ambassador to sue for peace.'

'Lou Chang recommends suing for peace,' said Yu the Vizier, 'and is of the opinion that, unless we do so, our armies face certain destruction in the field. But it will be Qin which calls the tune during the peace negotiations. In Your Majesty's estimation, is Qin in the position to be able to destroy our forces?'

'Qin is throwing all its manpower into this offensive,' said the King. 'Sooner or later it will overwhelm our armies.'

'If you take my advice, Your Majesty,' said Yu, 'you will send an ambassador with valuable gifts to establish diplomatic contacts with the states of Chu and Wei. They will be anxious to acquire your gifts and so will be certain to accept our ambassador. Once we have an embassy in Chu and Wei, Qin is bound to suspect a universal alliance against her interests. This is bound to cause alarm in Qin. Then and only then should we put out feelers for peace.'

Ignoring this advice, the King appointed his younger brother, the Lord of Pingyang, his negotiator, and despatched Zheng Zhu as an advance envoy to Qin, where his diplomatic credentials were accepted. Then the King summoned Yu the Vizier again.

'I have assigned my younger brother to negotiate with Qin, and they have already accepted Zheng Zhu as our envoy. What do you feel about this situation?' he asked.

'If negotiations fail to obtain an agreed settlement, then our armies face certain defeat,' replied Yu the Vizier. 'Qin will be chock-a-block with envoys from all over the world coming to congratulate her on her victory. Zheng Zhu is a man of some high standing. When he goes to Qin, the King of Qin and his prime minister, Fan Sui, Margrave of Ying, will reap world-wide propaganda capital from the negotiations. When Chu and Wei realise that we are suing for peace, they won't come to your rescue, Your Majesty. If they make no move to help you, we'll never be able to get Qin to negotiate peace.'

So as to impress the complimentary envoys, the Margrave of Ying indeed made much of Zheng Zhu, yet none the less he steadfastly refused to negotiate a peace. After the rout at Long Level, Handan was besieged, and its ruler became the laughing-stock of the whole world.

When Qin lifted the siege of Handan, the King of Zhao acknowledged Qin's suzerainty and appointed Zhao Shi to settle an agreement with Qin whereby peace was to be bought at the price of ceding the Six Counties region.'

'When Qin attacked our Kingdom,' said Yu the Vizier, 'did they go home because they were weary? Or do you really imagine they still had the strength to pursue their attack, but called it off out of loving consideration for Your Majesty?'

'When Qin attacked my Kingdom, they stretched their resources to the full,' said the King. 'They must have withdrawn from pure exhaustion.'

'Qin used all its resources to attack, failed to conquer us, and had to withdraw,' said Yu. 'If Your Majesty now makes them a present of what they couldn't conquer, that will merely be compounding their depredations on you. Next year when Qin launches another offensive against your Kingdom, there will be nothing to save you.'

The King reported Yu the Vizier's words to Zhao Shi.

'Is Yu the Vizier the final authority on the extent of Qin power?' retorted Zhao Shi. 'Does he really know the limits of Qin's resources for aggression? If we do not give this paltry thimbleful of territory, and if Qin renews the offensive next year, do you imagine that you'll be able to make peace then without first parting with your very capital?'

'If I were to cede the territory, as you suggest,' said the King, 'could you assure me that Qin won't attack next year?'

'I couldn't possibly assume the responsibility of guaranteeing you immunity from attack,' replied Zhao Shi. 'In the old days the neighbouring states of Hân, Wei, and Zhao were all on friendly terms with Qin. The reason why Qin is now well inclined towards Hân and Wei but attacks Your Majesty is that you have neglected to maintain such good relations with her. Now it is up to me to free you from the consequences of this attack occasioned by your shabby lack of friendship, and I shall have to smooth over the differences between our two states by an exchange of gifts, so as to put our friendship with Qin back on a par with that of Hân and Wei. If next year you alone are attacked, it will be because you will have been remiss in your conduct and attitude towards the Kingdom of Qin. It's not for me to guarantee you such a thing as outright immunity from attack.'

The King passed these words on to Yu the Vizier.

'According to Zhao Shi,' said Yu, 'if we don't obtain peace now, and Qin renews the offensive next year, we may very well have to cede even our metropolitan area in return for the cessation of hostilities. If we do negotiate peace, Zhao Shi still can't guarantee that Qin won't attack us again. So what's the good of ceding the Six Counties in any case? Next year we'll again have to sue for peace by offering them what they couldn't obtain by force. To me that's the best way of committing suicide. Better not to ask for peace at all. For all Qin's martial prowess can't win it the Six Counties. Even if Zhao can't put up an effective resistance, it will never lose this area for good by direct military conquest. Once Qin returns home battle-weary the war will cease.

'If we could use these Six Counties as a bait to induce the other states of the world to fight Qin to a standstill, we could be losing them to allies but gaining compensation at Qin's expense. Our nation would still gain some profit out of such a move. Isn't that better than just lounging back, doling out free gifts of territory to enfeeble ourselves and strengthen our enemy the Kingdom of Qin? Now when Zhao Shi talks about Qin favouring Hân and Wei and attacking Zhao, it must be because he thinks Hân and Wei will not come to Zhao's rescue and your armies will be left to fight on their own. Once you swallow the idea that you are to blame because of your lack of due respect to Qin, that will serve as an excuse for yearly pressure upon you to dish Qin up with six citadels until you've passively parted with all your territory. If Qin next year again expects you to cede territory, will you hand it over? For, if you don't, you will cancel out all this year's good-will and simply be inviting further disasters at the hands of Qin. If you do hand it over, you'll end up having nothing more to give away. For the saying goes; "The mighty are insatiably rapacious, the weak are incorrigibly submissive."

'If we meekly comply with our enemies' demands, they will increase their territory without any diminution of their armed might. There's no calling a halt in a policy which allows a steadily waxing Qin to lop territory from a constantly waning Zhao. There is, after all, a limit to your territory, whereas the demands of Qin are utterly boundless. If we cede our limited territory in response to their unlimited demands, soon you won't be able to find Zhao on the map any more.'

Before the King of Zhao had made up his mind as to which policy to adopt, a Zhao minister, Lou Yuan, came back from Qin to the court, where he and the King held counsel together.

'In your opinion,' said the King, 'is it advisable for me to give this territory to Qin or not?'

'Well, you see,' said Lou Yuan, trying to evade the question, 'I'm afraid my knowledge of the situation doesn't allow me to comment on that point.'

'I fully appreciate that,' said the King, 'but could you give me your personal opinion?'

'Your Majesty,' replied Lou Yuan, 'I assume you've heard of Gongfu Wenbo's mother? Gongfu Wenbo was a civil servant of the state of Lu. When he died of an illness, two of his womenfolk committed suicide in their apartments. At the news of these events his mother shed no tears at all. The funeral director expressed astonishment that she could remain so unmoved by the death of her own son.

' "The Master Confucius," replied the mother, "was such a noble-minded man that he once allowed himself to be driven from Lu rather than deny his principles. But this fellow, my son, didn't follow his example. He dies and two of his wives commit suicide. That makes it quite clear that he treated his parents shabbily, but went out of his way to please his women."

'Now there are two ways of looking at this. From the mother's own point of view, she was simply being a high-minded, virtuous mother. From the wives point of view, she was simply being jealous of them. Thus, though one and the same matter was under discussion, there could be two different points of view reflecting divergent attitudes towards it. Now here I am, just back from Qin. If I advised you not to give them the territory, that would constitute no positive advice at all. On the other hand, if I suggest that you *should* give them the land, I fear Your Majesty may suspect I am working for Qin. That is why I didn't dare answer your first question. But, just supposing I were in a position to advise Your Supreme Majesty, I would say it would be best to cede the Six Counties.'

'I am of the same mind,' replied the King.

When Yu the Vizier heard this, he entered the palace for an audience with the King.

'This is utterly specious talk,' he said. 'On no account should you cede these counties to Qin.'

News of Yu's admonition brought Lou Yuan hurrying back into the presence of the King, who passed on the gist of Yu the Vizier's view.

'He is wrong,' said Lou Yuan. 'Yu the Vizier has got hold of only one side of the argument. Why is it, do you think, that all the other States are delighted to see Qin and Zhao at loggerheads? Well, the rulers of the States say to themselves, "Let's line up with the strong to get what we can out of the weak." Now that our soldiers are being worsted by the Qin armies, all the complimentary envoys must already have turned up

LORD FLAT PLAIN

in the capital of Qin. So it would be best to make peace by ceding the land without further ado. In this way we'll make the other rulers believe that there is some pact between our country and Qin and at the same time we shall be appeasing Qin. Otherwise the rest of the States will take advantage of Qin's power and anger, and of our own debilitated condition, to slice us up like a melon. Do you suppose Qin's plotting alone is enough to encompass Zhao's destruction? That's what I mean when I say Vizier Yu only sees one side of the picture. Make up your mind here and now, Your Majesty, and don't go back on your decision.'

Once again Yu the Vizier got wind of this and straight away came to see the King.

'This is all terribly dangerous,' said Yu. 'Those efforts of Lou Yuan's on behalf of Qin will merely serve to awaken the suspicions of the other States while in no way appeasing the rapacity of Qin. Unfortunately he quite forgot to mention that we would be revealing our weakness to the other States. Besides, when I cautioned you against parting with the territory to Qin, it was not that I was against giving it away under any condition. If Qin demands the Six Counties from Your Majesty, you should bribe the Kingdom of Qi with them. In the light of the deep feud between Qin and Qi for the hegemony of the world, once Qi has the counties and is enabled to mount a multinational assault westwards against Qin, they'll agree to whatever you suggest before the words are hardly out of your mouth. Then what you've lost to Qi you'll recoup from Qin. If we go about it that way, Qi and Zhao can requite their long-standing hatred of Qin and demonstrate to the world that we are a force to be reckoned with. If you make it generally known abroad that you are in league with Qi, before your troops have even set foot on Qin's frontier, Qin, I think, will have sent heavy bribes to Zhao and be trying to buy a negotiated settlement from you instead of the other way round. Once Hân and Wei know that Qin is anxious to have good relations with you, they, too, will acquire a greater regard for our nation and are bound to compete with each other and race with costly treasures to be the first to purchase your friendship. In one move you will have gained the friendship of three countries and turned the tables on Qin.'

'Capital!' replied the King of Zhao.

Accordingly he sent Yu the Vizier eastwards to Qi, where joint discussions were held to devise opposition to Qin. Before Yu the Vizier had even returned home, the Qin ambassador was already in Handan, the capital of Zhao. Seeing how matters stood, Lou Yuan fled the country. The King of Zhao enfeoffed Vizier Yu with a walled city.

A short while later Wei asked to join in the alliance against Qin. The King of Zhao summoned Yu the Vizier for advice. Yu first called on Lord Flat Plain.

'I hope you will advise him in favour of the alliance, good sir,' said Lord Flat Plain. Yu the Vizier presently proceeded to the palace for his interview with the King.

'Wei is trying to conclude an alliance with us,' said the King.

'Wei is making a mistake,' said Yu the Vizier.

'But of course I haven't agreed to it,' replied the King.

'Your Majesty is making a mistake,' said Yu the Vizier.

'One minute you say Wei is making a mistake in asking for an alliance,' said the King, 'then the next you are saying I'm mistaken in not having accepted their overtures. Am I to consider the alliance advisable or not?'

'I have heard that if a little state collaborates with a large state, it's the large state that reaps the benefit if things go well, while the small state suffers the consequences if things go badly. Wei being a small state is inviting trouble, whilst Your Majesty with your powerful nation is failing to snap up a chance of possible benefit. That's why I say you're both making a mistake. In my humble opinion it *would* be profitable to conclude this alliance.'

After this advice the King approved the alliance treaty with Wei.

Later, when Yu the Vizier became involved with the disgraced Prime Minister of Wei, Wei Qi, in complete disregard of his own title as fief-holder of ten thousand rents and his seal of high office he preferred to abscond with Wei Qi, avoiding the wrath of Qin. Some while after they had left Zhao they found themselves embroiled in trouble in the capital of Wei. Wei Qi lost his life, and Yu, feeling himself a failure, took up writing to vent his disillusionment. For his subject-matter he went back to the Spring and Autumn Period, as well as making observations on the contemporary political scene. His works amounted in all to eight volumes, with such titles as *Code of Honour*, *Title and Privilege*, *Cogitations*, and *Statecraft and Diplomacy*. Since this last opus was a sardonic assessment of the changing fortunes of the various States, it has been known to posterity as *Master Yu's Interpretation of the Rise and Fall of Nations*.

Historical Commentary

Here follows the Grand Historian's commentary:

Simply because he lived in such a mean and sordid age, Lord Flat Plain stood out as a gaudy-feathered cockerel on a dung-heap. Yet the larger issues of life always eluded him.

'The thought of profit turns many a dizzy head,' runs the vulgar adage. In his greed for profit Lord Flat Plain listened to the evil offer of Feng Ting, thus sparking off the disastrous Long Level campaign in which Zhao lost its host of over four hundred thousand men, and its capital Handan nearly fell to the armies of Qin.

By contrast, what a master of clear thinking and complex subtleties Yu the Vizier revealed himself to be by the manner in which he assessed the political situation and formulated policies for Zhao. It was simply his human compassion for the disgraced Prime Minister Wei Qi that led him to grief in Daliang. Even a common fellow could have foreseen that such action would be courting disaster. How much more so a fine, intelligent man like Vizier Yu. All the same, if Yu had not plumbed the depths of sorrow, he would never have been able to write his books to reveal himself and his views to posterity.

Prince Fearless (Lord Trust Tumulus)

PRINCE FEARLESS OF WEI was the younger son of King Resplendent of Wei [295 – 277], and by a different mother the younger brother of King Peacebringer [276 – 243]. On the death of King Resplendent, King Peacebringer succeeded to the throne and enfeoffed Prince Fearless as Lord Trust Tumulus.

This was just after Fan Sui had fled from Wei to become Prime Minister of Qin. Because of his enmity towards the Wei minister Wei Qi, he had Qin forces lay siege to the capital of Wei, Daliang. They routed Wei's Third Army at Flowery Slope and put Chancellor Mang Mao and his troops to flight. The King of Wei and Prince Fearless were greatly distressed by the situation.

By nature the Prince was a kindly man and humble in his dealings with gentlemen; and, regardless of their merits, he always treated them with the utmost modesty and courtesy. Never once did he pull rank and wealth or treat them arrogantly. As a result, from thousands of miles around fine men came vying with each other to seek service under him, and he soon gained three thousand clients. Mindful of his outstanding qualities, and of the vast number of his retainers, the rulers of the other States did not dare launch military campaigns against Wei for a period of over ten years.

One day when Prince Fearless was playing chess with the King of Wei, news suddenly arrived that the alarm beacons had been fired on the northern frontier.

'Border raiders from Zhao are about to invade our territory,' said the messenger.

The King abandoned the game and was about to summon the Grand Council, but Prince Fearless restrained him.

'It's just the King of Zhao out hunting,' said the Prince. 'It's not an invasion.'

With this remark they resumed play. But the King was still nervous and his mind was not on the game.

A short while later another messenger came in with more news from the north.

'The King of Zhao is holding a hunt meet,' he said. 'It's not an invasion.'

'My lord,' said the King of Wei in utter astonishment, 'how on earth did you know that this was so?'

'Among my retainers,' replied the Prince, 'I have a man who is in a position to spy out the secret activities of the King of Zhao. Whatever the King does, this man immediately reports it to me. That's how I knew.'

After this experience, the King of Wei was so wary of the Prince's astuteness and ability that he dared not entrust him with any governmental responsibilities.

It happened that there was a certain recluse living in Wei called Hou Ying, who was about seventy years old. He was so poor that he took employment as porter of the Barbarian Gate of Daliang city. Prince Fearless came to hear of the presence of this anchorite in the city and went to the Barbarian Gate to invite him to take service in his household. But though he offered him generous gifts, the old man refused.

'I have maintained my personal integrity and been careful always to act with high a standard of morality all these many years,' he said. 'Just because I'm nothing but a gatekeeper and hard pressed to keep body and soul together, that's no reason why I should ever accept money from you, Your Highness.'

After this rebuff, the Prince prepared a great feast for all his retainers.

When all were seated, he drove off in his chariot, leaving the left-hand side place of honour vacant. It was his intention to go in person to fetch Master Hou Ying from the Barbarian Gate to the gathering.

Master Hou Ying straightened his tattered cap, adjusted his ragged coat, and without further ceremony or ado mounted the chariot. There he did not even bother to go through the polite motion of offering the seat of honour to the Prince, since it was his wish to watch Fearless's reactions. For his part, the Prince took hold of the reins and was only the more respectful towards him.

'I have a friend,' said Hou Ying, 'who's a butcher in the city market. I'd trouble you to drive over and pay him a call.'

Prince Fearless steered his chariot into the market place. Master Hou Ying alighted to greet his friend Zhu Hai the butcher. For a long while he deliberately stood there by his stall lingering in conversation, all the time watching the Prince out off the corner of his eye. As he unobtrusively observed him, he noticed that his facial expression merely increased in affability.

Meanwhile the whole hall full of generals, ministers, royal clansmen, and retainers was kept waiting for him to raise his cup and start the banquet. In the market the people were gasping at the sight of the Prince left standing there holding the reins of his chariot. His outriders were all secretly cursing Master Hou Ying. As Hou Ying still perceived no sign of impatience registered on the Prince's countenance, he took his leave and returned to the chariot. On their arrival at his residence Fearless ushered Master Hou to the seat of honour and, much to their consternation, introduced him to all his retainers.

At the height of the merry-making the Prince rose personally to toast his guest, Master Hou Ying.

'Your Highness,' said Hou Ying by way of reply, 'I've been mucking you around enough today. After all I'm nothing but the porter of Barbarian Gate, yet you put yourself out to drive over and invite me back to this vast assembly. It was quite inappropriate of me to ask you to call on someone on the way back, but you did me the favour all the same. With the further glory of your reputation in mind, I deliberately kept you waiting in your chariot there in the middle of the marketplace, and as I chatted to my friend, I kept an eye on you. As I did so, I noticed that your attitude only became all the more pleasant in spite of my deliberate procrastination. Consequently everybody there in the market concluded that I was a paltry, impertinent fellow, whilst you were a noble man willing to humble himself before one you considered a "gentleman of worth".'

At the conclusion of the feasting that night Prince Fearless welcomed Master Hou into his service as his chief client.

'That butcher Zhu Hai I called on,' Master Hou remarked one day, 'now, he's a fine man. Yet there's no-one around nowadays capable of recognising his ability. That's why he hides himself away among the butchers.'

On repeated occasions the Prince went to visit Zhu Hai to invite him to join his household, but, much to his mystification, the butcher did not even bother to express his refusal.

In the twentieth year of King Peacebringer of Wei's reign, when King Resplendent of Qin had defeated the Long Level Army of Zhao, his armies pressed on to beleaguer Handan. Now the elder sister of Prince Fearless was the wife of Lord Flat Plain, who in turn was the younger brother of King Benevolent Civility of Zhao. Repeatedly she had sent letters to the King of Wei and to her brother Prince Fearless begging for military aid. King Peacebringer sent his general Jin Bi in command of an army of a hundred thousand to relieve the State of Zhao.

At this development the King of Qin sent an emissary to Wei.

'I should point out,' this ambassador announced to King Peacebringer, 'that our campaign against Zhao is on the verge of success. A surrender is expected at any moment. Should any of the other States presume to offer aid and succour to Zhao, upon completion of our campaign we shall without fail divert our forces to an attack on that State.'

In his fear the King of Wei sent word to General Jin Bi to halt his troops and set up a fortified camp at Ye, still maintaining the pretext of going to the aid of Zhao, but in reality keeping both doors open while he watched further developments.

Lord Flat Plain sent a continuous stream of chariots bearing envoys to reproach Prince Fearless.

'The reason why I was willing to become in-laws with you,' he instructed them to say, 'was because of your lofty reputation for chivalry and justice, sir, and because you were known always to be ready to rush to the help of people in trouble. Now Handan is on the verge of falling to Qin no relief comes from Wei. Where's your readiness to help now? Even if you think nothing of me, and are prepared to abandon me to the mercies of Qin, you might at least have some pity for your elder sister.'

Taking this rebuke grievously to heart, the Prince personally petitioned the King several times that he might send relief to Zhao. At the same time he sent his retainers and professional rhetoricians to try and persuade the King by the manifold subtleties of their tongues. But the King feared Qin and persisted in refusing their advice.

Soon it dawned on him that he would never succeed in persuading the King, and he came to the conclusion that his own life was not worth preserving if he abandoned Zhao to certain destruction. So he gathered his followers about him and mustered a hundred or more chariots, intending to head out with his closest retainers to meet the Qin host and die fighting alongside the men of Zhao. As they passed the Barbarian Gate, they encountered Master Hou, and the Prince explained to him in detail why he was resolved to go to his death against the Qin armies. He bade his final farewell and made to set off on his journey.

'That's the spirit, Your Highness!' said Master Hou. 'I'm sorry this old fellow can't join you.'

After a few miles the depressing thought seeped through to Prince Fearless that things had not gone quite to his liking.

'I did everything I could for Master Hou. The whole world knows I did,' he thought: 'and that I'm about to die he hardly has a single

LORD TRUST TUMULUS

fond word of farewell to see me on my way. Tell me, where did I go wrong?'

He turned his chariot round and went back to have another word with Master Hou.

'I had a strong feeling you'd be back, Your Highness,' said Hou. 'Well now,' he went on after a pause, 'you are, to be sure, world-famous for your delight in the company of men of worth. But now that a spot of trouble has cropped up, just like that, without any other reason, you want to rush off headlong against the armies of Qin. You'll be like meat thrown to a hungry tiger. Just what are you trying to prove? Why bother to have retainers, then? You treated me generously, all right; yet, when you went off, I didn't even really bid you a proper goodbye, so of course I knew you'd take it to heart and come hurrying back again.'

In humble submission the Prince bowed twice and asked him for his advice. Master Hou bade the other retainers retire so that he might converse privately with him.

'I have heard that General Jin Bi's Tiger Tally of Authority is kept permanently in the King's bedchamber. Lady Compliance, the King's most favoured concubine, has free access to his bedroom, so it is well within her power to steal it. Now, I have heard that a long while ago, when her father was murdered, she for several years offered a reward to anyone able to avenge his death. From the King downwards everyone wished to try and avenge her father, but none succeeded in bringing the murderer to book. Lady Compliance wept before you, and you sent a retainer who managed to lop off the murderer's head, and you respectfully forwarded it to her. She would willingly die on your behalf, and certainly she would not refuse you any request. But so far the opportunity for expressing her gratitude has just not arisen. Just say the word to Lady Compliance, and she's bound to agree to anything you ask. So once you've got your hands on Jin Bi's tally you can seize control of his army and head north to Zhao, then drive Qin back towards the west. A master stroke, if you pull it off, worthy of the Five Great Hegemons of old.'

The Prince adopted his plan and asked Lady Compliance for her co-operation. She duly stole Jin Bi's tally of command and handed it over to the Prince.

As he was about to set out, Master Hou addressed him.

'When a general is out campaigning, there are occasions when he can, in what he deems to be the national interest, override even his ruler's orders,' he said. 'Even though you may try to take command in the usual way by matching your tally with that in Jin Bi's possession, if he is unwilling to hand over the troops to you and seeks final confirmation from the King himself, things could be rather dangerous. You might care to take my friend the butcher Zhu Hai along with you. He's a real hard man. If Jin Bi does as he's told, all well and good, but if he doesn't, you can let butcher Zhu Hai loose on him.'

At this the Prince burst into tears.

'Are you afraid of death, Your Highness?' asked Master Hou. 'Why all this crying?'

'Jin Bi is a roistering, boisterous old war-horse,' said Fearless, 'I fear that when I get there, he won't comply, and we'll just have to kill him. That's the only reason why I'm crying. My own death is not likely to bother me, is it, now?'

All the same he invited Zhu Hai to accompany him. The butcher laughed.

'I'm just a common-or-garden butcher only good for wielding a cleaver,' he said, 'but you've lowered yourself to visit me on several occasions before. The reason I never responded to your courtesy was that all I could have done for you by way of return seemed so piddling by comparison that it would just have been an embarrassment for you. Now that you're in a fix, the moment is right, and I'll risk my neck to repay your kindness.' So they set off together.

On the way they called in to thank Master Hou.

'I ought to go with you,' he said, 'but I'm old and past such things. By your leave I'll just count the days till I think you've reached General Jin Bi's army, then I'll turn towards the north and cut my throat by way of wishing you good luck in your enterprise.'

Prince Fearless set off.

When he reached the camp at Ye, he falsely claimed royal authority for replacing General Jin Bi. Though Jin Bi checked the tallies and found nothing wrong, he secretly had his own misgivings about the matter, and, scornfully waving a hand at the Prince, gave him a long, hard look.

'Here I am,' he said, 'with a hundred thousand men at my command, encamped on the frontier itself. It's a charge with enormous national responsibilities. And here you are turning up in a single chariot and trying to replace me. How about that for a bit of cool nerve?'

It was quite evident that Jin Bi had no intention of heeding the new orders. Zhu Hai had hidden a forty-pound steel mace in one of his copious sleeves. With this he maced Jin Bi into the ground. The Prince assumed command of the army and mustered his troops on parade to give them their orders.

'If any father and son are both present serving in this army,' he said, 'the father should return home: if any brothers are serving together, the elder should return: and if any only sons are present, they must go back to support their parents.'

In this way he was left with eighty thousand troops of high morale. These he led out to attack the armies of Qin. Qin retreated, thus relieving the siege of Handan and saving the fortunes of Zhao. The King of Zhao and Lord Flat Plain personally came to meet the Prince at the city boundary. Lord Flat Plain then in person bore the Prince's quiver of arrows and led the way, acting as his squire. The King of Zhao bowed again and again to Fearless in great humility.

'Never in the whole course of history,' he said, 'has any man ever matched your worth and noble integrity.'

From this time on Lord Flat Plain never dared again liken himself to Fearless. Meanwhile, after saying farewell, Master Hou Ying on the day he reckoned the Prince would have reached Jin Bi's army turned to the north, as promised, and cut his own throat.

Of course the Prince was well aware that the King of Wei would be furious with him for stealing his tally and for presuming to take such a drastic step as killing Jin Bi. After he had repelled Qin and saved Zhao he sent his generals back home to Wei with the army, while he himself stayed on in Zhao with his clients and retainers. For his part, King Perfect Filiality of Zhao thoroughly approved of the Prince's misuse of authority in having saved Zhao by assuming the command of Jin Bi's troops. In consequence of this he consulted with Lord Flat Plain and resolved to enfief the Prince with five walled cities. On hearing this news Fearless was overcome with pride, and showed in his bearing and air that he considered himself a great success. One of his clients decided to give him a piece of his mind.

'There are some things best forgotten,' he said, 'and some things which it's best not to forget. If someone does you a kindness, you should keep it in mind, but if you've done someone else a kindness, I'd suggest you'd best forget it. Quite apart from that general consideration, your flouting of the King of Wei's authority by seizing command of Jin Bi's army to save Zhao was no doubt of great benefit to Zhao, but as far as Wei is concerned you weren't exactly being a loyal subject. Frankly I wouldn't feel so pleased with myself, if I were you, or think myself such a top-notch success.'

At this Prince Fearless rebuked himself for his own folly and looked as if he wished the ground would open to swallow him up. The King of Zhao had the streets ceremonially swept and personally came out to welcome the Prince, honouring him with the ritual normally accorded to a monarch, and trying to lead him into the palace by the privileged route up the western steps. Fearless, however, stepped aside and politely declined, humbly insisting on ascending by the eastern steps. He confessed that the grave errors which he had committed by his ingratitude to Wei had cancelled out any meritorious service he might have rendered Zhao. At the ensuing feast, the King of Zhao helped him to wine all evening till night-fall, but in view of Fearless's self-effacing attitude he could not bring himself to mention the gift of five walled cities. In the end Prince Fearless decided to stay in Zhao, and the King gave him the demesne of Huo as his living. The King of Wei followed suit by presenting him with the fief of Trust Tumulus. In spite of this generous gift Prince Fearless still stayed in Zhao.

Prince Fearless heard that in Zhao lived two remarkable eccentrics. One was Master Mao, who lay low among the gambling fraternity, and the other, Master Xue, had gone to ground in a liquor shop. The Prince wished to interview the two. Both men, however, stuck to their privacy and refused to grant him an interview. By inquiry he got to know where they hung out and by circuitous methods managed to contact them. After lengthy continuous association he became the greatest of friends with these two men.

'Madam,' Lord Flat Plain one day said to his wife, 'I was given to understand that your younger brother, Prince Fearless, was a man without peer in this world. Now it comes to my ears that he has formed a most unsavoury relationship with gambling riff-raff and liquor vendors. The Prince is nothing more than a social misfit.'

His wife conveyed these remarks to her brother. Prince Fearless called round to take his leave of her.

'Dear sister,' he said, 'I was given to understand that Lord Flat Plain was a man of honour and worth, and that was why I turned my back on the King of Wei, to come and save Zhao in response to the summons of a worthy man. But it now appears that Lord Flat Plain associates solely with the high and mighty and makes no effort to seek out men of true worth. When I was in Daliang city back in Wei, I heard that these two men were fine fellows. My only fear was that on coming to Zhao I might not succeed in getting them to meet me. In view of the people I've been associated with in my life, it's a wonder to me that they should ever want to have anything to do with a person like me. If Lord Flat Plain finds this association disgraceful, surely it indicates he's not worth having in my company.' Whereupon he had his things packed in preparation to leave Zhao.

Lord Flat Plain's wife reported all that her brother had said to Flat

Plain. Head bared in humility, the lord came to make his apologies, trying his utmost to get the Prince to stay on. When Flat Plain's retainers heard of this incident, half of them left his service and joined Prince Fearless. Once again true men of mettle from all over the world flocked to the Prince. Before long he had emptied Flat Plain's household of clients.

Fearless did not return home, but stayed on in Zhao for ten years. When Qin heard that he was in Zhao, she time and time again launched attacks eastwards against Wei. Greatly perturbed by this course of events, the King of Wei sent emissaries to the Prince asking him to return. Prince Fearless was afraid the King still harboured anger against him.

'If anyone dares to act as intermediary for ambassadors from the King of Wei he shall die,' he warned his retainers. Even among those clients who had shared in his desertion of Wei by following him to Zhao there was not one single person who dared try to persuade him to return to his homeland. Master Mao and Master Xue went to see him.

'The high esteem accorded to you in Zhao,' they said, 'and the good name you enjoy throughout the other states of the world will last just as long as there exists a country called Wei. With Qin now attacking it, Wei is in a critical situation. If you are not concerned for Wei, and Qin destroys the capital Daliang and rases your ancestral temple to the ground, how will you be able to look the rest of the world in the eyes?'

At these words the Prince immediately flushed with shame and asked his charioteer to harness up with all due speed so that he might return to the assistance of Wei.

When the King of Wei met Fearless they wept together and he awarded the Prince the seal of office of Commander-in-Chief, which the Prince accepted. This happened in [247], the thirtieth year of King Peacebringer's reign. The Prince sent envoys to inform all the states that he was again in command, and on receiving this news the rulers sent generals with armies to the aid of Wei. He led forward the forces of the Five Allied Nations, Zhao, Hân, Qi, Chu, and Yan, which met and routed the Qin armies south of the Yellow River, putting even General Wild Stallion Meng himself to flight. They followed up this victory by pursuing the Qin forces right up to Box Valley Pass and hemmed them in so that they did not dare venture forth. Thereafter the Prince's prestige rocked the whole world, and unknown experts on strategy from the other states would come and proffer him their treatises on the arts of warfare. Unfailingly and generously he would lend such works his own name, which is why they came popularly to be known as *The Prince of Wei's Treatises on Warfare.*

The King of Qin was severely shaken by this course of events and laid out at least ten thousand pounds of gold to engage the services of retainers of the late General Jin Bi, bribing them to slander the Prince before the King of Wei.

'For ten years,' they said, 'the Prince was in refuge abroad, yet here he is commander-in-chief of the Wei forces with authority over all the generals of our allies, the Five Nations. The other heads of state bypass our King and pay attention only to the Prince. It is his intention to avail himself of this opportunity to usurp the royal prerogative and set himself up as king. Indeed all the other rulers are in such awe of his prestige that they are at this very moment in league to nominate him King of the Confederacy.'

Qin sent a number of *agents provocateurs* who pretended to have come to offer their congratulations, and then with affected innocence enquired whether the Prince had yet succeeded to the throne. Daily the King received news of such malicious slanders, and in the end he could not help but give credence to the rumours. Finally Qin's machinations bore fruit. The King sent someone to relieve Fearless of his command and take over the armed forces.

Fully aware that his dismissal was due to slander, the Prince simply excused himself from attending court, on grounds of ill-health. All night long he would sit up into the small hours drinking with his retainers. What he drank was the hardest of white spirits, and he lay very frequently with his women. For four years he caroused and drank day and night. In the end he succumbed to alcoholic poisoning: and in that same year King Peacebringer of Wei also died. On being informed of the Prince's death, the King of Qin sent Wild Stallion Meng to attack Wei. His armies ravished twenty walled cities, creating an occupation zone known as the Eastern Military Zone. Thereafter Qin proved a silkworm and Wei its mulberry leaf. Within eighteen years of Prince Fearless's demise Qin had taken the King of Wei prisoner and butchered the population of Daliang.

When the Illustrious Progenitor of our royal house of Han was a mere nobody, he often heard of the Prince's great ability. After he ascended the imperial throne, every time that he progressed through Daliang he never failed to make a sacrifice in reverential memory of Prince Fearless. In [195], the twelfth year of his reign, when he was returning from his campaign against the rebel general Ying Bu, the Tattoed One, he assigned five families for the upkeep of the Prince's tomb. For many generations after that there were seasonal sacrifices held in honour of the Prince.

Historical Commentary

Here follows the Grand Historian's commentary:

When I was passing through the ruins of the once great city of Daliang, I inquired as to the whereabouts of what they once called Barbarian Gate. This Barbarian Gate was in fact the eastern gate of the city.

LORD CHUNSHEN

There have been many lords and princes of this world who have delighted in the company of worthy gentlemen, yet Prince Fearless, in seeking out the company of troglodyte recluses and eccentric outsiders, was the man who really knew what he was doing. He considered it no shame to befriend the lowliest of men. It was for very sound reasons that his fame capped the world. Whenever the Illustrious Founder of our dynasty passed his tomb, he ordered the local people never to break off the tradition of sacrifice to the Prince's memory.

Lord Chunshen

LORD CHUNSHEN was a man of Chu State, called Huang Xie. He had travelled widely in the course of his studies and acquired considerable learning. Later he came into the service of Astute Perfection, King of Chu [298 – 263], who had a high regard for Huang Xie's rhetoric and mastery of the dialectic and sent him as his ambassador to Qin.

The King of Qin sent General Bai Qi to attack Hân and Wei, whose armies he defeated at Flowery Slope, capturing the Wei commander Mang Mao. Hân and Wei rendered submission and became vassals to Qin. Then King Resplendent of Qin ordered Bai Qi to join forces with Hân and Wei to attack Chu. Huang Xie, the Chu ambassador, had arrived in Qin just before the expedition was due to set out, and did not happen to hear of the plan until Qin had already despatched Bai Qi in advance against Chu. He captured Shaman and Black Centre provinces, took the cities of Yen and Ying, and pressed on to Border Tumulus. In the face of this invasion King Astute Perfection evacuated his government to Chen County in the east. Huang Xie recalled that King Cherisher of Chu had been gulled by Qin into going to her court. There he had been badly treated and detained till he died an exile in Qin. King Astute Perfection was the son of this unfortunate monarch, and for that very reason Qin despised him and calculated that one assault would be enough to wipe out Chu. Huang Xie sent a persuasive letter proffering advice to King Resplendent of Qin which went as follows:

There are no stronger states in the world than Qin and Chu. Now I hear that Your Majesty wants to attack and put paid to Chu – a situation resembling a contest between two tigers. After such fights jackals snap up the left-overs. Would it not be best to make friends with Chu? May I put forward my theory?

I have heard that things on attaining their extreme reverse their motion. The alternation of summer and winter is an example of this process. It is perilous to try to go beyond the limit. Piling up chequers is an example of this. With your territory extending right across the world from its eastern to its western confines you have achieved a situation unparalleled since the birth of mankind. None of the states able to muster ten thousand chariots ever gained so much. Since your early imperial predecessors King Civilisation [689 – 677] and King Solemn [613 – 591], generation after generation of your ancestors never lost sight of their aim of extending their territory right up to Qi in order to cut that state off from allies. Now, when you sent General Sheng Qiao to deal with Hân, he came back with their land in his pocket. It was a masterly stroke of yours to manage to gain a hundred miles of extra territory without bringing your armies into action or relying on bullying tactics. When on another occasion you did take military action and attacked Wei, you blocked up the gates of Daliang, seized the River Region, took the cities of Swallow, Sour Date, the Tombs, and Peach, and then entered Xing. The forces of Wei melted away like clouds and dared not come to the relief of these places. That was another great achievement of yours, Your Majesty.

You then ceased campaigning and rested your host for three years before renewing operations. By these operations you annexed Typha, Floodstream, Head, and Low Wall. Now you were in a position to menace Faith and Flat Top Hill, obliging the cities of Yellow and Fair North to man their defences. The house of Wei rendered you submission. Then Your Majesty cut off the territory north of Tinkle and the River Pu and occupied the key area between Qin and Qi. Thereby you broke the back of Chu and

Zhao. All the other states held conferences after conference and made alliance after alliance, but did not dare lift a finger to succour your enemies.

Your prestige now could not be higher. If you can maintain your successes and preserve your prestige, then the sage kings and powerful hegemones of the past will be unworthy to rank with you. Only by curbing your lust for conquest and consolidating the virtue of your government will you be able to preserve your prestige and avoid unhappy consequences in time coming. Instead you may choose to rely on the numerical superiority of your host and on the power of your weapons and chariots, and may seek to follow up the prestige which you have gained from the destruction of Wei by endeavouring to force all the world's rulers into vassaldom. But if you adopt any such course, the consequences, I fear, will be most unhappy.

> Everything has a beginning;
> an end is rarely achieved,

say the Odes.

> When a fox crosses water,
> its tail gets wet,

says the Book of Changes. The meaning of both remarks is that it's easy to start something but difficult to carry it through. How do we know this is so? Formerly the Zhi clan saw the profit to be had from attacking Zhao, but did not anticipate their disaster at Elm Row. Wu realised the advantage of attacking Qi, but did not foresee the defeat of Riverside Path. These two did not lack a previous record of great success, but they were simply blinded by immediate profit and underestimated the possibility of long-term disaster. Wu put its trust in the Kingdom of Yue and accompanied it in its campaign against Qi. On their return after the victory over the men of Qi at Mugwort Mound, the King of Wu was made prisoner by the King of Yue on the bank of Three Isles. The Zhi clan put its trust in Hân and Wei and joined with them to attack Zhao. They assaulted Sunlight City in Jin and were on the very brink of success when both Hân and Wei turned on the Zhi clan and slew Yao, Earl of Zhi, outside Grove Palace.

Now Your Majesty is resentful that Chu remains unconquered, but forgets that by destroying it you would be strengthening Hân and Wei. I think that, for Your Majesty's sake, it would be best not to adopt such a policy.

> A great army camps far from home,
> but does not cross the river,

say the Odes. And from this point of view the state of Chu should be your ally, whilst your neighbouring countries should be your enemies.

> The crafty hare may bound and leap,
> but even a stupid dog can catch it,

say the Odes. We should try and fathom out the way other people think. If, with your kingly mission only half accomplished, you now put your trust in the friendship of the princes of Hân and Wei, you will be doing the same as Wu did when it trusted Yue. I have heard it said:

> Enemies should be given no leeway,
> chances should not be let slip.

I'm afraid that although Hân and Wei repeatedly proclaim that they have your best interests at heart and are shielding you from trouble, their protestations are not sincere, and that in reality they mean to take underhand advantage of your great nation. Why do I think so? You don't exactly have a long record of doing favours to Hân and Wei. Rather they have quite a history of cause for resentment on their part.

In a continuous stream, their fathers and sons, elder and younger brothers, have met death at the hands of Qin for the past ten generations now. Their country is in ruins, their national altars to grain and soil, and their royal ancestral temples have all been destroyed. Their bellies have been ripped open, their tripes cut up, their necks broken, their jaws smashed, their heads parted from their bodies, their corpses and bones left exposed out in the marshy wilds and their skulls lying lifeless staring at each other along the frontiers. Fathers and children, elders and toddlers alike, all yoked by their necks and hands tied, have formed a continuous chain-gang of prisoners on the road. Their deserted ancestral spirits grieve alone, deprived of offerings and sacrifices. The ordinary people have no means of livelihood. The great clans have been dispersed and scattered, and their members have drifted into bondage all over the world as slaves and menials.

The fact that Hân and Wei have not yet been destroyed gives rise to anxiety about the survival of Qin itself. If you now assist them and join with them in attacking Chu, don't you think you'll have made a big mistake?

Moreover, if and when you mount your full attack on Chu, how exactly are your armies going to get there? Are you going to request right of way through Hân and Wei, whose populations are seething with thoughts of vengeance? When your troops set out through those lands, I think you'll have good cause to worry whether they'll ever return again. By such military operations you would only be playing into the hands of your enemies Hân and Wei. If you do not ask for right of way through Hân and Wei, who are so ill-disposed towards you, then you will have to attack the regions west of Compliant River. Now, that area is full of wide rivers and mighty torrents, mountains, forests, ravines and gullies – a land that will yield no provisions to you. Although you might overcome, you would not actually have obtained any territory. You would achieve the fame of having worsted Chu, but you would acquire no land and gain no real benefit, Moreover, the day you attacked Chu, the four other states would be bound to respond by proclaiming general mobilisation. With troops of Qin and Chu inextricably locked together in conflict, the house of Wei will set out to attack Rest, Fangyu, Sickle, Lake Mound, Patterned Stone, Xiao, and Xiang. This will lead to the complete obliteration of the State of Song.

Then the men of Qi will turn south to attack Chu. They are bound to *capture the upper reaches of Snot River, the most fertile region in the whole of the Great Plain, and thus Qi and Wei will be the ones to derive all the gain from the campaign. If Your Majesty conquers Chu, you will in doing so be making Hân and Wei the most prosperous of the central states and adding to the might of Qi. Hân and Wei will then have power sufficient to rival that of Qin. Qi will extend its southern boundary to Snot River. In the east it will have its back against the ocean, and in the north it will be able to depend upon the Yellow River as its frontier. It will have nothing further to worry about. There will be no stronger states in the world than Qi and Wei. They will ensure their national prosperity by expanding their territory. They may pretend to serve you as subordinates, but in a year or so, even if neither ruler calls himself emperor, they will have more than enough power to prevent Your Majesty from doing so. If, for all your extensive domains, vast population, and military might, you at one blow implant lasting resentment in the hearts of the people of Chu and cause Hân and Wei to support the claims of Qi to the imperial title, you will have gravely miscalculated in your planning.*

Thinking these things over from your point of view, Your Majesty, your best course would be to foster good relations with Chu. If Qin and Chu unite to put pressure on Hân, Hân is bound to drop any thoughts of conquest. If you avail yourself of the protection of the lofty cliffs of the Eastern Mountains, and the advantage afforded you by the Bending River, Hân will inevitably fall vassal to you. In that case, if you then station a hundred thousand troops in Zheng, the house of Wei will be filled with fear. The citizens of Xu and Yanling will lock themselves behind their city walls, and communications between Upper Grass and Shao Mound will be severed. In this way Wei, too, will become your vassal. As soon as you establish good relations with Chu, you will thus become lord over two of the most powerful nations and extend your territory right to the very frontiers of Qi. Without lifting a finger you can take the south-west part of Qi any time you like. Your territory will stretch from sea to sea, giving you mastery of the whole world. Then Yan and Zhao in the north will be unable to come to the aid of Qi and Chu in the south and east. Neither will be able to offer any help to the other. And by putting the frighteners on Yan and Zhao you will

LORD CHUNSHEN

immediately shaken Qi and Chu. These four nations will fall into line before they're even hurt.

'Marvellous advice,' said King Resplendent. Then he called off Bai Qi's campaign, dismissed the envoys of Hân and Wei, and sent ambassadors to Chu with financial inducements for an alliance with that nation. Huang Xie formally accepted the alliance and returned to Chu.

The King of Chu sent Huang Xie and Completion, the Crown Prince, to go as hostages to Qin, where they were kept for several years. When King Astute Perfection was taken ill, the Crown Prince was not allowed to return. He was, however, on good terms with the prime minister of Qin, Margrave Ying. So Huang Xie set about trying to talk the Margrave round.

'Premier,' said Huang Xie, 'are you really a good friend of the Crown Prince of Chu?'

The Margrave assured him he was.

'I fear,' said Xie, 'that the King of Chu will not recover from his illness. The best thing for Qin would be to send the Crown Prince home. If he manages to ascend the throne, he will be generous in his service of Qin and infinitely grateful to you, Premier. By befriending him and giving him a nation, you will in effect be gaining a state backed by ten thousand chariots. If, however, you fail to send him home, then he will be a commoner in rags hanging about in your capital Xianyang here. For in that case Chu will simply crown another prince in his place. Then you can guarantee that the new King will not be likely to do Qin a goodness. By failing to give him his nation you will be throwing away the chance of good-will from a powerful state backed by ten thousand chariots. That would be a grave miscalculation. I'd like you to think things over very carefully.'

Margrave Ying passed these suggestions of Xie's on to the King of Qin.

'First,' said the King of Qin, 'send the Crown Prince's tutor on ahead to inquire about the King of Chu's illness. On his return we shall make further plans.'

Huang Xie now proposed a scheme to the Crown Prince.

'The reason why Qin is detaining you,' he said, 'is that she hopes for some gain. But you don't have it within your power to provide them with any gain. I find that most disturbing. The Lord of Yangwen and his two sons are in the capital of Chu. Should His Majesty pass away, you will not be on the spot, so of course one of Lord Yangwen's sons will succeed to the throne. You will not then be able to carry out your hereditary state duties and obligations to your ancestors. It would be best for you to flee from Qin along with the envoys accompanying your tutor. I beg to be allowed to stay here and pay for your escape with my life.'

The Crown Prince disguised himself as a charioteer and drove the Chu envoys out through Box Valley Pass, while Huang Xie stayed in his residence, constantly feigning illness as a pretext to absent himself from the Qin court. Once the Crown Prince was beyond the reach of any possible pursuit by Qin, Huang Xie went in person to explain matters to King Resplendent.

'The Crown Prince has already left,' he said, 'and is a good way off by now. I deserve death. Will you kindly oblige?'

Mightily enraged, the King was on the point of granting the right of suicide, when Margrave Ying intervened.

'Xie was just doing his duty as a minister,' he said. 'His very function demands devotion to his master's cause. When the Crown Prince succeeds to the throne, he is certain to want to employ Xie as a high-ranking minister. For this very reason it would be advisable to let him return home unpunished, just to acquire the good will of Chu.'

So the King of Qin let Xie go. Within three months after he reached Chu, King Astute Perfection died and Crown Prince Completion succeeded him on the throne. He was the ruler known as King Complete Ardour [262 – 238]. In the first year of his reign he made Huang Xie his Prime Minister, enfeoffing him as Lord Chunshen and bestowing on him the twelve counties north of the River Huai.

LORD CHUNSHEN

Fifteen years later Huang Xie spoke one day to the King of Chu. 'The region north of the River Huai,' he said, 'lies along the frontier with Qi. It's a dangerous location. May I have your permission to incorporate my twelve counties into a military zone?'

Permission was granted, and Lord Chunshen amalgamated the counties into a military zone, which he presented to the King, at the same time requesting another fief in the Yangtse hinterland of Chu. King Complete Ardour assented to this. Lord Chunshen proceeded to establish his citadel and capital on the ruins of the ancient capital of the Kingdom of Wu.

While Chunshen was Prime Minister of Chu, Lord Mengchang was active in Qi, Lord Flat Plain in Zhao, and Lord Trust Tumulus in Wei. All were vying with one another for able followers and desperately competing for the services of retainers and clients to further the interests of their respective nations and maintain their own power.

In the fourth year of Lord Chunshen's premiership Qin smashed Zhao's Long Level army of more than four hundred thousand troops. In the next year they laid siege to the Handan, capital of Zhao, and in this crisis Handan solicited support from Chu. Chu sent Lord Chunshen to Zhao at the head of a relief army, and he did not return till the armies of Qin had withdrawn.

In the eighth year of Chunshen's premiership Chu campaigned in the north, destroyed Lu, and made the philosopher Xun Qing governor of Orchid Mound. At this time Chu was undergoing a period of national revival, and it was now that Lord Great Plain sent an emissary to Lord Chunshen, who lodged him in his most splendid apartments. This Zhao envoy wished to show off in Chu, so he wore tortoiseshell hairpins and adorned his sword-scabbard with pearls and jade. He asked to be considered an honorary retainer of Lord Chunshen. There were more than three thousand retainers in the service of Lord Chunshen, and when they attended the reception for the envoy of Zhao, all the most prominent of them were wearing pearl-studded shoes. The envoy was thoroughly discountenanced.

In the fourteenth year of Chunshen's premiership King Solemn

Perfection [249 – 247] ascended the throne in Qin, made Lü Buwei his Chancellor with the feudal title of Margrave Refinement and Trust, and conquered Eastern Zhou.

In the twenty-second year of Chunshen's premiership the various rulers of the States, dismayed by Qin's incessant predatory attacks, made alliances with one another to march westwards and campaign against Qin. It was the King of Chu who was made leader of this confederacy, but the whole management of operations was in Lord Chunshen's hands. When the confederate forces reached Box Valley Pass, the armies of Qin issued forth and utterly routed them. King Complete Ardour put the blame on Lord Chunshen, who consequently fell steadily from favour.

Now among Chunshen's clients there happened to be a man from Lookout Ford named Zhu Ying.

'Everybody,' he said to Lord Chunshen, 'makes a great deal of the might of Chu but underestimates your contributions to the growth of that power. This seems all wrong to me. In the old days you managed again and again for twenty years to create good relations with Qin, and she did not attack Chu. But shall I tell you the real reason why there was no attack? Well, it would have been rather awkward for the men of Qin to come over by way of Toad Gulch Pass to attack us here in Chu. Nor could they have taken a short cut through the two Zhou states, which would have left them open to attack from the rear by Hân and Wei.

'Times have certainly changed, haven't they? Wei can fall any time now – they can't even hold on to Xu or Yanling any more. If the State of Wei is annexed by Qin, then Qin will be within just fifty miles of Chen. As I see things, the fight between Qin and Chu can come any day now.'

As a consequence of Zhu Ying's advice Chu evacuated the population of Chen to Longevity Spring. But then Qin moved the population of Wey to Wild King to set up the Eastern Military Zone. After this Lord

LORD CHUNSHEN

Chunshen went back to his fief down in Wu and from there continued to carry out his governmental duties as Premier.

King Complete Ardour of Chu had no sons, which occasioned Lord Chunshen great anxiety. He sought out a large number of nubile and fecund young women and presented them to the King. Still no sons were born. Li Yuan, a man from Zhao, brought his younger sister along to present her to the King of Chu. But hearing that the King was not very potent, he feared it would be a long time before she received the royal favours. So he sought employment as a retainer of Lord Chunshen. In going for an interview with Lord Chunshen he missed his appointment with the King, so he went back and paid Lord Chunshen another visit. Chunshen asked what had happened.

'The King of Chu sent messengers round to ask for my younger sister,' he replied: 'I had one or two drinks with them and missed my appointment.'

'Has she been formally betrothed to the King?' asked Lord Chunshen.
'Not yet.'
'Mind if I have a look at her, then?'
'Not at all.'

Thereupon Li Yuan introduced his younger sister to Lord Chunshen. After Chunshen had lain with her, it presently became evident that she was pregnant. Li Yuan plotted with her and she seized an opportunity to try to win round Lord Chunshen with her persuasive tongue.

'The King of Chu treats you with such favours,' she said, 'even greater than those accorded any one of his own brothers. But although you have been Premier for over twenty years, all this time the King hasn't had any heir born to him, so even he if lives to over a hundred, it will still be one of his brothers they are bound to appoint as his successor. Whoever his successor is, he is bound to favour and honour his own particular familiars. Then how will you manage to stay in favour? What I'm telling you now is not just a lot of airy-fairy talk. You've been at the helm for a long while, and during that time you've often insulted the King's brothers. So if any of his brothers does indeed ascend the throne, disaster will overtake you. What chance will you have of hanging on to your seal of office or your fief in the Eastern Hinterland? Now, I know I am pregnant, but no-one else knows, and it wasn't long ago that you made love to me. If you, with your powerful influence, were to present me to the King of Chu, he would be bound to favour me in his bed. If Providence has vouchsafed a son in my womb, then that son of yours will one day become the next King. Wouldn't it be better to get your hands on the whole of Chu than to lay yourself open to who knows what fearful, vindictive punishments?'

The Lord of Chunshen found himself in thorough agreement with her proposal. He removed her from his own quarters, installed her in the 'Apartments of Chaste Seclusion' and mentioned her to the King of Chu. The King summoned her into his seraglio and granted her body the royal favours. She duly bore a son, who was made Crown Prince. His mother became royal consort. Li Yuan was accorded high esteem by the King, and considerable power came his way.

Once Li Yuan had secured the position of royal consort for his sister and that of Crown Prince for her son, he felt afraid that Chunshen might divulge the truth about her pregnancy and become increasingly bold and troublesome. Secretly he built up a suicide squad of knights with the intention of using their murderous services to silence Lord Chunshen once and for all. But news of the plot became common knowledge throughout the land of Chu.

Lord Chunshen had been Prime Minister for twenty-five years when King Complete Ardour fell ill. One day Zhu Ying spoke to Lord Chunshen.

'There is unpredicted good fortune,' he said, 'and unpredicted disaster. Now, my lord, you find yourself in an unpredictable age serving an unpredictable ruler. So how can you get by without that unpredicted helper who can cope with the unpredicted and unpredictable?'

'Just what do you mean by unpredictable good fortune?' asked Chunshen.

'You've been Prime Minister for over twenty years,' said Zhu Ying. 'In name you're only the Prime Minister; but in reality you're the King of Chu. The titular King is ill and about to expire any day now. Then, as Prime Minister to a minor, you'll be able to take over the regency, just as Yi Yin and the Duke of Zhou did of old. So that when the new King attains his majority and comes to actual power, if he should fail to co-operate, then you have only to make a public announcement of your undeniable right to be King of Chu in name as well as actuality. That is what I mean by unpredicted good fortune.'

'And what about unpredicted disaster?' asked Chunshen.

'Because Li Yuan has not acquired the premiership, he nurses deep ill-will towards you, sire. It is not for military ends that he has been training a suicide squad. When the King dies, he's certain to step in and *putsch* the palace and kill you to ensure your silence. That's what I mean by unpredicted disaster.'

'And that leaves the unpredicted helper?' said Chunshen.

'Sire, you should instal me as an officer of the Palace Guard. When the King of Chu dies, Li Yuan is sure to make his move, and it will remain only for me to kill him. That's what I mean by an unpredicted helper.'

'My good sir,' said Chunshen, 'put such thoughts out of your mind! Li Yuan is a weak, ineffectual man. Besides, I've been good to him. Why on earth should things come to such a pass?'

When Zhu Ying realised that his suggestions were not going to be adopted, he feared that he would be caught up in the imminent disaster and made good his escape.

Seventeen days later King Complete Ardour of Chu died. As predicted, Li Yuan stepped in and carried out his *putsch*. He deployed his suicide squad in ambush behind Halberd Gate, and when Chunshen entered the palace, the killers moved in on him, ran him through, and cut off his head, which they tossed outside the Gate. Next Li Yuan sent officers to wipe out the whole of Chunshen's family.

The boy sired by Chushen and born of Li Yuan's younger sister after her presentation to the King now ascended the throne. He was known as King Profound of Chu [237 – 228].

That same year was the ninth in the reign of the First Emperor of Qin [246 – 210]. In Qin, Lao the Rake debauched the Empress and caused a great scandal. His debauchery came to light and his whole clan was exterminated. Lü Buwei, his patron, was also ruined.

Historical Commentary

Here follows the Grand Historian's commentary:

When I went to the region of Chu, I saw the old city walls and palaces of Lord Chunshen. What a splendid sight! Earlier in his career, when Lord Chunshen used his persuasive powers on King Resplendent of Qin and risked his own life to secure the safe return home of Chu's Crown Prince, he showed enormous intelligence and perspicacity. Later, when he allowed himself to be manipulated by Li Yuan, he was senile and past it. As the saying goes:

> Settle things when they should be settled,
> or they will settle you.

This admirably sums up Lord Chunshen's neglect of Zhu Ying's counsel.

ASSASSINS

Cao Mo

CAO MO, a man from the state of Lu, was of great courage and physical strength, and thus came into the service of the ruler, Duke Solemn [693 – 662], who admired such qualities. He was put in command of Lu's armed forces and in battles with the Kingdom of Qi was thrice defeated and put to flight. Alarmed by this, Duke Solemn sought to obtain peace at the cost of ceding the demesne of Fulfilment to Qi. Nevertheless he still retained Cao Mo as commander of his forces.

Duke Mighty Order of Qi [682 – 642] agreed to meet the ruler of Lu at Axehandle to make a treaty. After they had both solemnised their pact on a raised ritual terrace, Cao Mo with a dirk in his hand suddenly menaced the Duke of Qi. Since none of his close attendants dared so much as make a move, the Duke tried questioning his assailant.

'What might it be you require from me?'

'Admittedly Qi is strong, and Lu is weak,' replied Cao Mo, 'but your great nation has gone too far in its violation of our country. If you destroy the defensive walls of Lu, then a buffer against your greater enemies will have been removed and the pressure will be on your own frontier. You might just think that over, my lord.'

Duke Mighty Order promptly agreed to return to Lu all the territory which he had previously conquered. Once the Duke had given his word, Cao Mo immediately threw away his dirk, descended from the terrace, paid his loyal respects, and went to his place among the other officials, showing no change in his facial expression and engaging in casual conversation as before. Duke Mighty Order was enraged and had every intention of breaking his agreement.

'No, that won't do,' said his great minister Guan Zhong. 'To display such niggardly covetousness and personal indulgence is to throw away the confidence of the rulers of the other states and lose us support throughout the world. You'd be best advised to return them their territory,'

Heeding this advice, Duke Mighty Order ceded Lu its conquered lands, and the area which Cao Mo had lost in his three battles was all restored to Lu.

Zhuan Zhu

One hundred and sixty-seven years afterwards there occurred the affair of Zhuan Zhu in the Kingdom of Wu. Zhuan Zhu was a native of Hall Land county in Wu. When Wu Zixu fled from Chu to Wu, he got to know of Zhuan Zhu's great ability. After gaining an audience with King Handsome of Wu [526 – 515], Wu Zixu tried to persuade the King of the advantages of attacking the Kingdom of Chu.

'This fellow Wu Zixu,' cautioned Prince Light, 'had a father and a brother who both met their deaths at the hands of the King of Chu. His suggestion that we should launch a campaign against Chu is designed to accomplish his own personal vendetta and cannot possibly be intended for our advantage.'

The King of Wu went no further with the matter.

Wu Zixu learned that Prince Light had long nursed the secret desire to do away with King Handsome.

'Prince Light must have his eyes on the throne,' concluded Wi Zixu. 'The time is not yet ripe for me to try to influence foreign policy.' With this in mind he recommended Zhuan Zhu into the Prince's service.

Prince Light's father was the former King of Wu, Zhufan [560 – 548], who had three younger brothers, the first called Yuzhai, the second Yimo, and the youngest Youngest Son Zha. King Zhufan realised that Youngest Son Zha was a man of great ability, so he did not set up his Crown Prince as his successor, but instead decreed that the succession should pass to each of the brothers in turn, calculating that Youngest Son Zha would thus eventually succeed to the throne anyway. On the

ZHUAN ZHU

death of Zhufan the throne passed to Yuzhai [547 – 531]. After him it passed to Yimo [530 – 527]: and then it should have been Youngest Son Zha's turn. But he was of another mind and fled the country to avoid assuming his responsibilities, so the people of Wu set up Yimo's son Handsome instead.

'Supposing the succession went by order of brothers, then Youngest Son Zha should be King,' was Prince Light's reaction. 'But if we were to resort to succession by sons, then I am the legitimate heir and should be King.'

Thinking in this way, he made it his business secretly to take under his wing gentlemen of keen intellect and cunning enterprise to further his ambitions for the crown. When he acquired the services of Zhuan Zhu, he accorded him excellent treatment as one of his own retainers.

Nine years afterwards King Pacifier of Chu [528 – 516] died. In the following spring King Handsome, wishing to take advantage of the death of the Chu monarch, sent his two younger brothers the Princes Gaiyu and Zhuyong at the head of troops to lay siege to the city of Qian in Chu, and also sent Youngest Son Zha, now Lord of Long Tombs, to the neutral state of Jin, where he was to observe in diplomatic circles the other rulers' reactions to these developments. Chu sent troops to cut off Gaiyu's and Zhuyong's lines of retreat, preventing the armies of Wu from returning.

'This is too good an opportunity to miss,' said Prince Light to Zhuan Zhu on hearing this news. 'Nothing ventured, nothing gained. Besides I am the true heir apparent and ought to be King. Even if Youngest Son Zha returns, he won't depose me.'

'I would say,' suggested Zhuan Zhu, 'that it would be quite a viable proposition to kill the King. His mother is old and his children mere infants. His two younger brothers are trapped with their armies in Chu.

ASSASSINS

At this juncture the King of Wu, having embroiled himself in serious trouble abroad in Chu and being left with no faithful champions here at home, just couldn't touch us.'

'I value your life as I do my own,' said Prince Light, kowtowing his thanks to Zhuan Zhu for this advice.

One day [between 7 March and 5 April 515 B.C.] Prince Light had mailed knights concealed in one of his cellars and held a wine feast to which he had invited King Handsome. The King providentially positioned his troops along the road from his palace to Prince Light's residence, where his own clansmen were stationed by the steps and doorways. They lined his route with long two-edged swords in their hands.

At the height of their feasting, Prince Light feigned a twinge of gout and excused himself from the company. Then he went down to the cellar where he instructed Zhuan Zhu to conceal a dirk inside a grilled fish and serve the fish to the King. Once he was in front of the King, Zhuan Zhu split open the fish, snatched up the dirk, and stabbed the King to death on the spot. Those in close attendance upon the King then slew Zhuan Zhu, after which the King's men fell into confusion. It was at this point that Prince Light chose to spring his ambush and set his armoured knights upon the King's followers who were slain to a man.

So it was that Prince Light made himself monarch, the King whom we know as Helü [514 – 496]. He enfeoffed Zhuan Zhu's son and made him his Prime Minister.

Yu Rang

WHAT FOLLOWS NOW took place some seventy years later and concerns a man called Yu Rang, a native of the State of Jin. He had served two of the six great feudal clans, Clan Fan and Clan Zhongxing; but his service with them did nothing to advance his reputation, so he left them and took up employment with the Earl of Zhi, chief of Clan Zhi, who treated him with great honour and favour. When the Earl of Zhi attacked Viscount Accomplishment of Zhao, head of Clan Zhao, the latter joined with the clans of Hân and Wei to plot the Earl's annihilation. This fulfilled, they divided up his territory between the three of them. It was Viscount Accomplishment of Zhao who hated the Earl most of all. Such was his lingering animosity that he had his skull lacquered and made into a drinking vessel.

'Bitter fate,' cried Yu Rang, who had escaped and fled into the mountains. ' "A gentleman will lay down his life for a true friend as gladly as a lady preparing her body for her true love." The Earl of Zhi was a true friend to me. I will give my life if necessary to avenge him. For only if I avenge him will my spirit rest without shame.' He changed his name and assumed the identity of a convict labourer. Eventually he managed to find employment in the palace, white-washing the privy. On his person he had concealed a dagger with the intention of stabbing Viscount Accomplishment. As the Viscount approached the privy, his heart beat quickly, as if in premonition, and he had his men seize and interrogate the convict labourer white-washing the privy walls. It was, of course, Yu Rang, and they discovered the knife concealed on him.

'It was my ambition to avenge the Earl of Zhi!' he shouted out. Those in attendance on the Viscount wished to kill him, but the Viscount restrained them.

'He is a man of faith and honour,' explained Viscount Accomplishment. 'I shall merely be very careful to keep out of his way in future. The Earl of Zhi is dead and gone without a single living relative left. Yet his minister still wants to avenge him. Why, this must be the noblest man in the whole world.' So in the end he let him go free.

Shortly afterwards Yu Rang daubed his body with lacquer to give himself leprous sores and scabs, swallowed charcoal to make himself hoarse like a dumb person, and contrived to conceal the true form of his body. When all this had been done, he went begging in the market. There his wife passed him by without even recognising him. But as he made his way round the town, he met with a friend who did recognise him.

'Aren't you Yu Rang?' he asked.

When Yu Rang admitted that he was, his friend started to weep.

'With your great ability, if you went to Viscount Accomplishment, gave him gifts as token of your allegiance, and took up service with him, he would certainly treat you as an intimate favourite. In such a position wouldn't it be much easier to do what you desire? Why inflict such torture and suffering upon your body in this way? Doesn't it make your quest for vengeance all the more difficult?'

'To kill someone to whom one has sworn allegiance,' replied Yu Rang, 'would be the basest treachery. Besides, I have deliberately chosen the most difficult way. The reason why I have done so is all the more to shame any future would-be traitors to their lords.'

Shortly after Yu Rang's encounter with his friend, Viscount Accomplishment was due to make a public appearance. Yu Rang hid beneath a bridge on the route he was to take. But as the Viscount approached the bridge, his horse shied.

'It must be Yu Rang there,' he said.

He sent his men to investigate, and, sure enough, they discovered Yu Rang.

'Didn't you once serve Clans Fan and Zhongxing?' the Viscount reproached him. 'Both were massacred by the Earl of Zhi. Yet did you once think of avenging them? No, on the contrary you went and swore fealty to the Earl himself. Now he too is dead. So why persist in your obsession with avenging him?'

'When I served Clans Fan and Zhongxing,' replied Yu Rang, 'they treated me as one of the common herd. So I repayed them as one of the herd would have done. But it was different with the Earl of Zhi. He treated me as one of the nation's élite. So as one of the élite I tried to repay him.'

'Alas,' said the Viscount with a deep sigh and his eyes welling with tears, 'Master Yu, by what you have done for the Earl of Zhi you have already made a great name for yourself. But to have received our pardon once is sufficient. Now defend yourself as best you can, for I cannot let you go twice.'

The Viscount ordered his soldiers to surround him; and as they did so, Yu Rang shouted to him, 'I have heard it said that an enlightened lord does not begrudge others their due fame and that a loyal minister has the moral duty to die for his good reputation. By your magnanimity in pardoning me once before, you have earned universal praise for your nobility. As for today, I shall certainly submit to execution, but may I first ask you, my lord, for your coat so that I may slash at it and demonstrate before the world my vengeful intention? Grant me this, and in death I shall bear you no grudge. Not that I dare expect you to grant this request. I am merely expressing a pious hope.'

Full of admiration, the Viscount bade someone hand over his coat. Yu Rang whipped out his sword and sprang three times at the coat slashing at it with his sword.

'Now I can go down to Hell and report to the Earl of Zhi!' he said. Then, falling on his sword, he died. On the day of his death all true gentlemen of honour throughout the nation of Zhao wept at the news.

Nie Zheng

IN THE KINGDOM OF WEI some forty years later there lived a man called Nie Zheng. He dwelt in Deep Well Ward in the city of Axlehead. To avoid a vendetta after he had killed a man he made his way with mother and elder sister to the kingdom of Qi, where he took up a livelihood as a butcher.

Some while afterwards, the nobleman Yan Zhongzi of Puyang city, capital of Wey, was serving under the ruler of Hân, Margrave Righteous [399–387], and quarrelled with Xia Lei, the Prime Minister of Hân. Fearing execution, he fled the country and travelled through many lands in search of men who might help him avenge himself on Xia Lei. When he was in the Kingdom of Qi, someone mentioned that Nie Zheng was a gentleman of great courage and was lying low in the butcher's quarters to avoid the consequences of a vendetta. Yan Zhongzi called on him in person several times. On one occasion he arranged a party at which he himself waited upon Nie Zheng's mother with the wine. At the height of the feast he went over to Nie Zheng's mother and tried to make her a present of a hundred ounces of gold. Nie Zheng was amazed at his generosity and firmly refused the gift. Yan Zhongzi was most insistent, but Nie Zheng persisted in his refusal.

'I have an old mother, you see, bless her. We're very poorly off, and I've come here to foreign parts to make my living as a dog-butcher. That's how I manage to provide a few delicacies and fine clothes for her daily needs; and since my place is here providing for all she needs, I really can't accept your kind offer.'

Yan Zhongzi took him aside to explain.

'I have an enemy on whom I wish to avenge myself,' he said, 'and my quest for vengeance has taken me to many a kingdom, but all to no avail. When I arrived in Qi, I heard that you were a man of great faith and honour, and that is why I offered you this trifling sum, as a meagre contribution towards the upkeep of your dear mother and in order that I might earn your friendship. Naturally this doesn't give me the right to make further demands on you.'

'The only reason why I turned my back on higher ambitions and degraded myself by coming to live amongst the butchers in the market-place,' replied Nie Zheng, 'was simply that I might stay near my old mother and look after her. While she's still in the land of the living, I could hardly pledge myself to anyone else.'

Yan Zhongzi repeatedly tried to overcome his objections, but he remained adamant. In spite of that, Yan Zhongzi accorded his hosts all due courtesy before leaving.

With the passing of years Nie Zheng's mother finally died. The funeral over and the period of mourning at an end, Nie Zheng became very thoughtful.

'A sad business,' he sighed, 'Here I am just one of the market riffraff, hacking up meat all day. Yet there's that Yan Zhongzi, a great minister at one time to one of the Kings, trapesing all this way to try and make friends with a fellow like me, and all his trouble for nothing. And what a miserable way I treated him. I have never done a single thing worth mentioning to match his generosity. He tried giving me a hundred ounces of gold for my mother. Granted I didn't accept, but it was simply his way of showing me he valued me as a true friend. When a great man like Yan Zhongzi, with his mind seething with lofty schemes of noble vengeance, comes personally knocking at the door of an utter nobody like me, can I just sit back and do nothing? When he asked me to help him that time, I was completely wrapped up in my old mother's well-being. Now that the old lady, bless her, has passed peacefully away after a good full life, I shall definitely try to make myself useful to so fine a friend.'

With such thoughts in mind he headed west for Puyang, and there he sought out Yan Zhongzi.

'The reason why I declined to help you before, Master Zhongzi,' he said, 'was solely that my old mother was still alive. But now that the good old lady has gone to rest, may I ask on whom it was that you wanted to revenge yourself? Perhaps I could help you to put the matter right.'

ASSASSINS

Yan Zhongzi told him everything down to the last detail.

'My enemy is none other than the Prime Minister of Hân, Xia Lei. Now, he happens to be the uncle of the ruler of Hân, he has a host of clansmen, and his residence is bristling with bodyguards. The number of times I've had my men go in there to run him through . . . ! Not one of them has been able to pull it off. But now, sir, what a stroke of good fortune that you still remember me. Might I possibly put some more chariots, horsemen, and armed knights at your disposal to help you on your way?'

'Hân and Wey are right on top of each other,' answered Nie Zheng. 'If we are going to kill the prime minister of a neighbouring state, and especially when he's related to the monarch himself, the last thing needed for the job is a crowd of people. If I go with a whole gang of men, some of them are bound to fall out. Once people fall out, they have a tendency to open their mouths too wide. If they start talking, you'll have the whole State of Hân as your deadly enemies, and that could well prove dangerous!' So he declined the offer of armed support, took his leave, and set off for Hân with only his sword for company.

Xia Lei, Prime Minister of Hân was sitting in state in the upper end of the hall of his residence surrounded by a mass of armed men with weapons at the ready. Nie Zheng marched straight in, mounted the steps, and stabbed him to death. In the panic and confusion that followed, Nie Zheng, roaring ferociously, cut down a few score of the body-guard. Next he set about peeling the skin from his own face, gouged out his eyes, slashed open his stomach, and pulled out his entrails. So died Nie Zheng.

The Hân authorities had his unrecognisable, mutilated corpse exposed in the market-place, and tried by the inducement of a monetary reward to establish its identity. In vain. Next they put up 'WANTED' notices throughout the land promising a reward of a thousand pieces of gold to anyone able to come forward with information as to who the assassin was. Time passed, and still they learnt nothing.

NIE ZHENG

Nie Zheng's elder sister, a lady called Prudence, heard that somebody had stabbed the Prime Minister, that the murderer could not be identified, and that in spite of exposing the assassin's corpse and offering a reward of a thousand pieces of gold, the authorities had been unable to discover his name.

'Can it have been my little brother?' she sobbed bitterly, 'For wasn't he befriended by Yan Zhongzi?'

Without further delay, she set off to the market-place of the capital of Hân: and there, as she had feared, the corpse turned out to be her brother's. She threw herself down on his body and wept piteously.

'That's him they called Nie Zheng, from Deep Well Ward in the town of Axlehead. That's who he is,' she cried.

'This man did violence to our Prime Minister,' exclaimed some of those amongst the milling crowd in the market-place. 'Surely this woman must know that the monarch has offered a reward to anyone who can reveal the identity of the corpse. Woman, how on earth do you dare publicly own that you know him?'

'I'm well aware of all that,' she replied. 'But the only reason Nie Zheng ever bemeaned himself to go and live among the common tradesmen of the market-place was that our dear mother was still alive and well, and I hadn't found myself a husband. When our mother came to the end of her days and I was married off, what else could Nie Zheng do, after Yan Zhongzi had raised him from the dirt and so generously numbered him among his friends? It's true what they say, that a gentleman must be prepared to lay down his life for a friend. It was only because I was still alive that he mutilated himself beyond recognition, so as to leave no clues behind that could implicate his relatives. But I'm more afraid of my brother never getting known for the great man he was than I am of losing my own life.'

The market crowd were utterly astounded. She gave three great cries of 'Heaven have mercy on me!' and amid bitter sobs died of grief there by her brother's side.

When the news spread through the lands of Jin, Chu, Qi, and Wey, there was one universal judgement; 'Nie Zheng was not the only one in that family who possessed outstanding calibre. His sister too was a true heroine,' everyone declared.

If Nie Zheng had known in the first place that his elder sister would have no inclination to keep things quiet and would not be overawed by the prospect of having her corpse exhibited in the market-place, but would rather instead brave the cruellest dangers to ensure his due fame and die alongside him in the market of the capital of Hân, then he might well never have been so rash as to put his person at the disposal of Yan Zhongzi. But Yan Zhongzi certainly knew how to choose the right friend and recognise a true knight when he saw one.

Jing Ke

Now let us turn to the incident of Jing Ke, which took place some two hundred and twenty years afterwards in the Kingdom of Qin. He was a man of Wey whose ancestors had moved there from Qi. At the time when some forefather of his took up residence in Wey, the populace there dubbed him 'Squire Qing,' for Qing was the only typical Qi surname they knew. But later, when Jing Ke moved on to the State of Yan, those northerners there mispronounced this name as 'Squire Jing', meaning 'Squire Thorn'. Jing Ke was a well-read man and a skilled swordsman, and he tried to sell himself by these abilities to Lord Origin of Wey, which state was a vassal of Wei; but Lord Origin was not interested. Later when Qin attacked Wei and set up the administrative zone known as the Eastern Military Zone, she transferred Lord Origin of Wey and his followers to the city of Wild King.

Once when Jing Ke was travelling round the various states in quest of employment, he passed through Elm Row, where he discussed fencing with the famous swordsman Ge Nie. During this discussion Ge Nie glared angrily at him, and Jing Ke went away. Someone said he should try and call Jing Ke back.

'Just now when I was discussing fencing with him, there was something we disagreed about, and I gave him a hard look. Go and look for him if you like, but he's sure to have made himself scarce. He wouldn't dare hang around here.'

In the end he did send a messenger to Jing Ke's lodgings, but he had already harnessed up his chariot and left town.

'He was bound to have left,' said Ge Nie, when the messenger brought him this news, 'After all, I glared at him, didn't I?'

On another occasion, when Jing Ke's travels took him to Handan, capital of Zhao, he had a game of backgammon with the master swordsman Lu Goujian. A move was in dispute. Lu Goujian lost his temper and bellowed angrily at his opponent. Jing Ke made off without muttering a word in return, and they never met again.

When Jing Ke moved to the state of Yan, his dearest friends were the dog-butchers and Gao Jianli, a great dulcimer-player. Jing Ke was an inveterate tippler, and day in, day out, he would be drinking in the market place of the capital with Gao Jianli and the dog-butchers. When the drinking was in full swing, Gao Jianli would strike up his dulcimer, and Jing Ke would sing to his music there in the middle of the market, purely for their own entertainment. Then, moved to tears, they would weep together, for all the world as if there was no-one else around. Yes, it is true that Jing Ke hobnobbed with drinking men, but all the same he was a dedicated scholar and lover of learning, and in every country he made good connexions with all the most worthwhile people. In Yan, for instance, he was well received by that distinguished recluse the Venerable Tian Guang, who recognised him as not of the common sort.

Some time later it happened that Cinnabar, the Crown Prince of Yan, who was a hostage in Qin, fled back to his own native land. Now, he had originally been a hostage in the State of Zhao. King Righteous of Qin had been born in Zhao, and in his childhood he and Prince Cinnabar had been close friends. When Righteous ascended the throne of Qin, Cinnabar became hostage in Qin. In spite of their former relationships, the King of Qin treated his hostage discourteously, which infuriated Cinnabar and occasioned his flight. On his return he nurtured schemes of revenge against the King of Qin, but Yan, being such a small state, could do little against the might of Qin. Later, when Qin was daily launching more and more campaigns east of the Bean Mountains against Qi, Chu, Hân, Wei, and Zhao, steadily whittling away at the territories of the other states just as a silkworm nibbles away at mulberry leaves, the state of Yan, too, was menaced and its King and Government feared that the worst was to come. Filled with anxiety, Crown Prince Cinnabar asked the advice of his Grand Tutor, Ju Wu.

'Qin's territory spans the world. It menaces Hân, Wei, and Zhao. In the north it enjoys the impregnable defences of Sweet Springs and Valley Mouth. In the south it controls the fertile reaches of the Rivers Jing and Wei and dominates the rich lands of Ba and Han. On the west it is flanked by the mountains of Kansu and Szechwan, and on the east by the precipitous defiles of Box Valley Pass and the Bean Mountains. It has large resources of population, knights noted for their fierce prosecution of war, and a superabundance of armaments. If it is minded to launch an attack, then there is no place south of our Great Wall and north of our Waters of Change which we could hold against their hosts. Simply because you're resentful at having been insulted is no reason to go ruffling the scales of that dragon.' This was Ju Wu's advice.

'What action can I take, then?' asked the Prince.

'Let me think that one over, if I may,' replied his tutor.

Shortly afterwards the Qin general Fan Wuqi offended his King and fled to Yan, where the Crown Prince received him and kept him on as a guest in his house.

'That won't do at all!' remonstrated Ju Wu. 'The King of Qin is such a violent man that I shudder to think what will happen if ever he loses his temper with Yan. And think how much worse it will be if ever he discovers the whereabouts of General Fan! It is simply casting meat in the path of a hungry tiger, simply inviting inevitable disaster, from which even crafty Guan Zhong and wily Yan Ying of old could not extricate us. I would prefer you to send General Fan right away to find refuge in the land of the Huns and thus remove any pretext Qin might use for invading us. I would further have you form an alliance in the west with Zhao, Hân and Wei, and in the south with Qi and Chu. In the north we should link up in some way or other with the Hunnish Khan. Then, and only then, can we consider measures against Qin.'

'My dear Grand Tutor,' said the Crown Prince, 'if I do as you suggest, it will drag things out indefinitely. I'm at the end of my tether, and I fear I can't wait a moment longer. That's not the only reason. General Fan is without a friend in the world and has sought refuge with me. I could never think of abandoning a friend in need and packing him off to those Huns just because Qin is breathing down my neck. The hour has come to make or break me. I must ask you to think again, my dear Grand Tutor.'

'It does no good,' said Ju Wu, 'to pursue contentment by stirring up crises or to chase after happiness by creating calamities, especially when one's plans of revenge do not do justice to one's overweening resentment. To stick to one newly-made friend to the detriment of the common weal of the whole nation is inviting disaster by pandering to one's personal emotions. Your efforts would be like using a goose-feather to stoke up a stove of glowing charcoal – all to no avail. And what will happen if the predator of Qin is moved to acts of rage and violence doesn't even bear thinking about. There is a certain Venerable Tian Guang here in Yan, an astute and valorous gentleman, whose counsels you might seek.'

'Grand Tutor,' asked the Prince, 'might I avail myself of your good offices for an introduction? I would like to become his friend.'

'I would be honoured to oblige,' replied the Tutor. He sought out the Venerable Tian and told him that the Crown Prince wished to consult his opinion on matters of statecraft. The learned doctor readily consented, and made his way to the palace, where the Crown Prince came out to welcome him and, himself shuffling backwards as a token of his respect, led him into the palace. Once inside, the Prince knelt and personally brushed down the sitting-mat of honour. When Tian Guang was seated and everyone else had retired, the Crown Prince courteously approached him.

'Venerable sir,' Prince Cinnabar addressed him, 'Qin or Yan has to fall, either one or the other. I should be grateful for your considered opinion.'

'I have heard it said that a racing steed in its prime can gallop a thousand miles in a day, but when it's old and tired a jaded hack can outpace it. It is the reputation I acquired in my youth that you have heard of, and you don't realise how old age has sapped my energy and spirit. But though I would not presume to apply myself to matters of state, my much respected friend Jing Ke might undertake the task.'

'My dear sir,' replied Prince Cinnabar, 'might I rely on your good offices to gain me Squire Jing's friendship?'

Tian Guang readily assented, rose, and hastened out of the palace. The Crown Prince saw him to the gate.

'Sir,' he cautioned Tian Guang, 'what I have told you and what you have said constitute important state secrets. I beg you not to divulge them.'

'Have no fear,' said Tian Guang, bowing, and smiling to himself.

Suddenly a bent old man, he made his way to Squire Jing.

'Everybody in Yan knows that you and I are good friends,' said Tian Guang. 'Aware of my youthful reputation and not realising that my physical powers were no longer up to the mark, the Crown Prince kindly sought my assistance. He is convinced that there can be no peaceful existence between Qin and Yan, and sought my opinion. I found it impossible entirely to wash my hands of the affair, and took the liberty of putting forward your name. I wonder if you would be so good as to pop over to the palace.'

'I'm only too glad to oblige,' said Jing Ke.

'As I know it,' said Tian Guang, 'a superior man leaves no room for suspicion in his conduct. Just as I was leaving the Crown Prince, he enjoined me that what we had discussed was a matter of national security and that I should on no account divulge it. From this I deduce that the Crown Prince has doubts about me. To attract the suspicions of others through one's behaviour is contrary to the code of a loyal and chivalrous gentleman.' He hoped by taking his own life now to spur on Jing Ke.

'Please go quickly and see the Crown Prince and tell him that I have died to assure him of my silence.' With these words he cut his own throat and died.

When Jing Ke arrived before the Crown Prince, he informed him of Tian Guan's death and passed on his words. Twice the Prince bowed low in reverent memory, then went down on his knees, and crawled around weeping and sobbing. It was some while before he could find words.

'My warning the venerable Tian to keep his silence was simply because I didn't want anything to spoil the realisation of my great enterprise,' he said after some while. 'Never for one moment did I imagine that the dear worthy gentleman would kill himself to demonstrate his discretion.'

When Jing Ke was seated, the Crown Prince rose from his seat, walked over, and respectfully kowtowed before him.

'The Venerable Tian, unaware how unworthy I am,' he said to Jing Ke, 'afforded me this opportunity to meet you and speak with you. This is fate's way of showing compassion to the land of Yan, not abandoning it like an orphan child. Qin is a rapacious nation, and there is no limit to its greed and ambition. Its desires will not be satiated until it has swallowed up the whole world and made vassals of all the kings within the seas. It has already captured the King of Hân and seized all his territory. It has launched massive campaigns against Chu in the south, and in the north it is coercing Zhao. The Qin general Wang Jian is assailing the southern borders of Zhao with an army of several hundred thousands, whilst their General Li Xin is launching attacks from Grand Plain and Middle Clouds and marching through the western regions of Zhao. Zhao cannot stand up to the Qin onslaught and is bound to become a vassal state. When that happens, Yan will be faced with disaster. We are a small, feeble nation and have often been worsted in war. In my estimation all the resources of our country are no match for Qin. With the rulers of the various states all under the heel of Qin there is no hope of renewing the former Vertical Alliance against that mighty nation. Now my own private plan is briefly as follows.

ASSASSINS

'What I need is the services of one of the world's most valiant knights to go as my envoy to the land of Qin to win the confidence of its ruler by offering him rich presents. For this King of Qin is a greedy fellow and the offer of gifts will assuredly purchase us the opportunity we have longed for. If my envoy is able to menace the King of Qin with personal violence and persuade him to return all the conquered lands to the other rulers, as Cao Mo did with the Hegemon of Qi, Duke Mighty Order, then that will be a great blessing to the world. If the King fails to concede the territories, my envoy can simply cut him down. Once the King is dead, with his great generals and their armies still abroad as they are and with the turmoil that will ensue in the capital, the Government of Qin will be plagued with uncertainty. This will be the opportunity for all the rulers of the other states to renew the old Vertical Alliance and the destruction of Qin, once and for all, will then be assured. That is my most cherished wish: but I do not know to whom I can entrust the task. All I ask of you, Squire Jing, is to favour me with your opinion.'

There was a long silence before Jing Ke gave an answer.

'This is grand politics,' he said. 'Somewhat beyond the range of an old broken warhorse like me. I rather fear I'm not up to the task.'

The Crown Prince went right up to him and kowtowed, begging him not to decline. At last Jing Ke assented. The Prince honoured him by making him his highest minister, housing him in the most splendid quarters. Daily he would call upon him with gifts of the finest fare, showering him with rare and costly objects. At frequent intervals he would send him chariots with outriders and beautiful women for Jing Ke to indulge his desires, so that he might foster his good-will to the cause.

Time passed, but still Jing Ke showed no inclination to set out on his mission. Meanwhile the commander-in-chief of Qin's armies, General Wang Jian, had smashed the State of Zhao, captured its King, and annexed all its territory, and was now advancing northwards devouring all the land right up to the southern frontiers of Yan itself. In fear and dread the Crown Prince invited Jing Ke to visit him.

'Any time now,' he said, 'the Qins will be fording the Water of

Change. Although I would love to entertain you here indefinitely, my dear sir, I fear that the situation may not allow it much longer.'

'You have taken the very words out of my mouth, my dear Crown Prince,' replied Jing Ke. 'I was just about to broach the subject myself. But if I don't go with the right sort of presents, it will be difficult for me to convince Qin of my *bona fidè* intentions, and then I won't be able to get near the King of Qin. Now about our General Fan Wuqi.... You know, I suppose, that the King of Qin has put a price on him of two thousand pounds of gold and a fief of ten thousand rents. If I could only present General Fan's head and some maps as a title-deed for our fertile border-region of High Watch as gifts to the King of Qin, then he would be bound to be delighted and give me an audience. And then I will be in a position to repay your kindness.'

'General Fan came to me for help when he was in desperate straits,' said the Crown Prince. 'I could never allow my personal desires to harm anybody I respect. Please think of some other way, will you?'

Realising that the Prince would never resort to his plan, Jing Ke paid a secret call on Fan Wuqi.

'I must say, general,' said Jing Ke, 'the King of Qin's treatment of you has been abominably vile. He had your parents, family, and clan all wiped out or reduced to slavery. And it's come to my ears that into the bargain they've now put a reward on your head of two thousand pounds of gold and a fief of ten thousand rents. What on earth is one to do about it all?'

Wuqi looked up to Heaven in supplication, gave a great sigh, and started to weep.

'It's very much on my mind all the time,' he said, 'and it grieves me to the very marrow of my bones. But rack my brains as I will, I still can't hit upon a plan of revenge.'

'If the troubles of Yan and your own quest for vengeance could be dealt with by one word, what would you say to that?' asked Jing Ke.

Wuqi moved closer to him.

'What is there that we can do then?'

'General,' said Jing Ke, 'would you be so kind as to give me your head as a present for the King of Qin? He will be so pleased to see it that he will grant me a personal audience. Then with my left hand I shall grasp his sleeve and with my right plunge my dagger into his chest. In this way your vengeance will be accomplished, and the shame of the humiliating wrongs and abuses our nation has suffered will all be eradicated. But of course I can hardly expect you to agree to such a proposition.'

Fan Wuqi rolled up a sleeve and clenched his wrist with the other hand in a gesture of frenzied eagerness and leant forward towards Jing Ke.

'Do you realise,' said the General, 'that I've been grinding my teeth and rotting my heart out night and day just for a chance like this?' At last you've shown me the light.'

With these words he cut his own throat.

When the Crown Prince heard the news, he rushed over and prostrated himself on the corpse, weeping most brokenly. But since there was nothing that he could do to remedy the situation, he had General Fan Wuqi's head encased and sealed in a casket.

Now, the Crown Prince searched throughout the world for the sharpest of dirks, and for a hundred pieces of gold obtained a dagger from the famous collector Xu Furen of Zhao. He made his artificers temper the blade in poison. Then he tried it out on people. At the first scratch which produced the merest trickle of blood they died immediately. Next he had everything packed for Squire Jing's departure. In Yan there lived a valiant knight called Qin Wuyang, who had killed his first man at the age of twelve. He was a fearsome fellow, and nobody dared so much as give him an ugly look. The Crown Prince made him Jing Ke's assistant. Jing Ke was waiting for someone else to join him whom he wished to take as his companion, but the man lived a long way away and he had still not arrived when everything was all ready for the departure. After a while, seeing that Jing Ke had still not set off, the Crown Prince became impatient, thought that he was procrastinating, and wondered whether he was having second thoughts. So he invited him round again.

'Time is running out,' he said. 'I imagine you're not in the mood just now. Would you mind if I sent Qin Wuyang on ahead?'
Jing Ke was furious and bellowed at the Crown Prince.
'It's not for you to send anyone off, Crown Prince,' he said. 'It's a stupid dolt who plunges into a venture without considering how he's going to achieve it, let alone going into an immeasurably powerful country like Qin with just a dagger in his hand. The reason why I've been delaying is that I've been waiting for one of my retainers whom I wanted as my companion. Since you imply I'm procrastinating, let me take my leave here and now.' With that, he set off on his journey.

The Crown Prince and those of his retainers who knew about Jing Ke's mission went to see him off, all wearing the white clothes of mourning. When they got to the far side of the Waters of Change they performed sacrifices to the god of the road, drank wine, and chose his route to Qin. Gao Jianli played the dulcimer, and Jing Ke sang to his tunes, which were in a minor key. All the knights present wept and sobbed. Then Jing Ke stepped forward and sang this song:

> *By the wintry Waters of Change, alas!*
> *the bleak winds moan,*
> *where a bold knight sets out, alas!*
> *never to return.*

Then he sang in another mode, a spirited, impassioned tune which brought a fierce light to the eyes of all those knights and made their hair bristle with fury beneath their hats. Then he mounted his chariot and set out with never so much as a backward glance.

On arrival in Qin he made a lavish present of goods and money worth a thousand gold pieces to the palace chamberlain Meng Jia, one of the Emperor's favourites, and the Chamberlain put in a good word for him by way of introduction to the Emperor.

'The King of Yan is truly overawed by Your Majesty's might,' said the Chamberlain; 'nor does he dare mobilise his troops to oppose your generals, but rather would offer you his country as a vassal state and be numbered alongside the other princelings, to pay you tribute and taxes like any of your own internal administrative cantons and be allowed to continue his sacrifices to his ancestral temple. In his dread he does not dare to come and explain this to you in person, but respectfully sends you a sealed box with the head of Fan Wuqi and also proffers you maps of the southern regions of Yan. He renders his respects from his court, sends you these gifts, and entrusts a messenger to convey his communications to you. He awaits Your Majesty's command.'

The King was delighted at this and arranged a grand ceremonial reception at court to receive the Ambassador of Yan in Xianyang Palace.

Jing Ke bore the sealed box containing the head of Fan Wuqi, while Qin Wuyang followed behind with the casket of maps. When they came to the foot of the steps leading to the throne, Qin Wuyang grew pale with fear and began to tremble, which aroused the suspicions of the assembled ministers. Jing Ke looked back, smiled at Qin Wuyang, and apologised to the King.

'Whenever a miserable savage from beyond the pale of civilisation sees the Son of Heaven for the first time, he's bound to get into a state of nerves. I beg you, Your Majesty, to put up with him for a while until he's completed his mission.'

'You hand me the maps Wuyang is holding!' the King replied. Jing Ke took out the maps and presented them. The King started looking through the maps, and when he came to the last one, the dirk was suddenly revealed. With his left hand Jing Ke seized the King's sleeve and stabbed at him with the dirk in his right. The King became alive to the danger before the dirk could reach him, and jumped to his feet, jerking himself away so violently that the sleeve was ripped off. He tried to draw his own sword, but, since it was a long one, he had to grasp the scabbard. In the panic of the moment, and because the sword was tight, he couldn't draw it straight away. Jing Ke pursued him, and in his desperate attempt to escape the King dodged round a pillar.

All this happened so quickly and unexpectedly that the ministers were completely stupefied and robbed of all initiative. Moreover, under the rigid Qin protocol all ministers and attendants were forbidden to carry even the smallest weapons in the Palace and the officers of the Imperial Guard who did bear weapons were all disposed at the other end of the hall and could only approach the King when summoned. At the height of the crisis the King had no respite to summon the guards, which gave Jing Ke the chance to pursue him. The royal lackeys had nothing with which to attack the assassin, and in their panic they buffeted him with their bare hands. It was at this moment that the court physician Xia Wuju hurled the medical bag he was holding at Jing Ke. While the King was dodging round the pillar, and the lackeys were in a panic with no idea what to do, one of his courtiers shouted out, 'Your Majesty, swing your scabbard on to your back, you'll get a better pull.'

The King followed this advice, managed to draw his blade to counter-attack, and slashed through Jing Ke's left thigh. Crippled by this wound Jing Ke raised his dirk and threw it at the King. It missed and hit the bronze pillar. With renewed courage the King assailed him and wounded him in eight places. Now Jing Ke realised that his endeavour had failed. He leaned back against a pillar and gave a laugh. Then he slumped down into a contemptuous squatting position and reviled the King.

'Where I went wrong,' he said, 'was in wanting to keep the King alive and force him to make an agreement which I could take back to the Crown Prince.'

The courtiers now advanced and despatched him. But it was some time before the King of Qin regained his equanimity. When he did, he assessed the varying degrees of reward due to the ministers and those others present. To the medical man Xia Wuju he gave four thousand eight hundred pieces of gold.

'Wuju really loved me,' he declared. 'He threw his bag of medicines at Jing Ke.'

Enraged by these events, the King of Qin redoubled his military campaigns against Zhao and ordered General Wang Jian to lead his forces against Yan. In the tenth month of that year they took Thistle

City, capital of Yan. King Joyful of Yan [254 – 222], together with Crown Prince Cinnabar and others, withdrew their crack troops to take up defensive positions in the Liaodong Peninsula. There the Qin general Li Xin harried the King of Yan's forces relentlessly. Prince Admirable of Dai [227 – 2], last ruler of the royal house of Zhao, wrote a letter to the King of Yan;

It is because of your Crown Prince Cinnabar that Qin harries you so vigorously. If you kill Cinnabar and present his head to the King of Qin, he will certainly make peace with you, and you will be able to maintain your ancestral line and continue your sacrifices to the former members of your house.

Some time after this, when General Li Xin was pursuing the Crown Prince, the Prince went into hiding in the region near the River Billow in Liaodong. The King of Yan now at last sent envoys to execute the Crown Prince, intending to present his head to the King of Qin. Despite this, Qin renewed its attacks against Yan and five years later finally destroyed the nation, making its king captive. It was in the following year that Qin swallowed up the whole civilised world and the King of Qin assumed the title of Emperor.

So thorough was the pursuit and rooting-out of Crown Prince Cinnabar's retainers and associates and those of Jing Ke that they were all driven into hiding.

Gao Jianli changed his name and became a common labourer, working clandestinely in Songzi. One day, after many years of grinding toil, he happened to hear a guest playing the dulcimer in his master's hall. He loitered around outside, unable to drag himself away from the music.

'That's all right . . . but that's not so good,' he kept on saying every now and then. Other servants reported it to his employers.

'That labouring fellow seems to be an expert on the dulcimer,' they said, 'he's playing the secret music critic.'

The head of the house summoned him before them to play the

dulcimer. His performance elicited the praise of all present, and he was rewarded with wine.

Now Gao Jianli could see no other end to the humiliating obscurity and conditions of restraint which he had borne so long; so he begged leave to retire from the company. Then he took out his dulcimer and his finest robes, which he kept packed in his trunk. When he rejoined the company he was totally transformed in appearance. All those present were astounded, rose from their seats to accord him the courtesy due to a social equal, and treated him as an honoured guest. They invited him to sing and accompany his song upon the dulcimer. Not one left that gathering without tears flowing down his cheeks. One after the other the gentry of Songzi invited him to be their guest. Soon his reputation reached the ears of the First Emperor of Qin, who summoned him to appear before him. On his arrival at court one of the Emperor's staff recognised him.

'Why, that's Gao Jianli,' he exclaimed. Because the Emperor treasured Gao's virtuosity on the dulcimer, he was particularly lenient on this occasion and contented himself by merely having Gao Jianli's eyes blinded with the smoke of burning horse-dung. On every occasion thereafter when he had him play his dulcimer the Emperor never failed to applaud.

As time passed the Emperor gradually allowed him closer to him. Gao Jianli loaded his dulcimer with lead, and finally, when asked to play once more, he managed to come right up to the Emperor, near enough to lash out at him with the dulcimer. He missed. This time the Emperor had him put to death; and for the rest of his life he never allowed any of the retainers of the deposed rulers into his presence.

When Lu Goujian heard of Jing Ke's attempt on the Qin monarch's life, he said to himself;

'What a tragedy! It's a pity he was so slapdash with his knife-play. What an absolute failure I myself am at recognising good men when I see them. When I yelled at him that time, he must have concluded that I was beneath all human worth.'

ASSASSINS

Historical Commentary

Here follows the Grand Historian's commentary:

In many of the current traditions about Jing Ke which talk of Crown Prince Cinnabar and his fate mention is made of 'heaven raining grain' and 'horses growing horns.' Such incredible nonsense is too much to swallow. It is also wrong to suggest that Jing Ke actually wounded the Qin monarch. Gongsun Jigong and Master Dong Zhongshu were once on friendly terms with Xia Wuju and learnt all the true facts from him. They in turn passed them on to me as I have set them out in the above account.

Of these five men from Cao Mo to Jing Ke some succeeded in their noble design while others failed, but this much they all shared in common: they left the world in no doubt as to the nature of their intent, nor were they found traitors to their lofty aspirations. It is truly no foolish quirk of fate that their names have survived and that their fame continues to endure throughout the ages.

JESTERS

'THE SIX CLASSICS,' Confucius remarked, 'share one thing in common – they all have a good moral effect. The *Book of Rites* lays down the rules for social behaviour; the *Book of Music* fosters harmonious social dispositions; the *Book of History* provides beneficial historical precedents; the *Book of Odes* helps to perfect the expression of thought; the *Book of Changes* explains cosmological phenomena; and the *Spring and Autumn Annals* encourages adherence to objectively based morality and loyalties.'

At this point, I the Grand Historian, would also like to put in a word. Nature is so copious that there is room enough for everything, so why don't we expand on Confucius's remark? Even a joke or a witty turn of phrase can do a good job in solving some of the world's knotty problems and tricky situations.

Baldy Chunyu

BALDY CHUNYU, a man of Qi, had the misfortune to live with his in-laws. He was less than five feet tall, but had a sharp wit and quick tongue. For this latter reason he was several times sent as an ambassador to other states and was never once worsted in diplomatic debate.

King Awesome of Qi [356 – 319] was fond of riddles and cryptic word-games. He also loved lewd and lascivious entertainments and all-night drinking sessions. He was so pickled in alcohol that he neglected his governmental duties and left everything to his grand ministers. Sheer chaos reigned throughout his administration, and other states were for ever encroaching upon his frontier territory. The nation was on the verge of complete and utter ruin. None of his courtiers dared suggest he should mend his ways. But Baldy Chunyu attempted to reason with him by means of a riddle.

'There's a big bird in this land who has settled on the royal palace and for three years it hasn't flapped its wings or uttered a single peep. Does Your Majesty know what sort of a bird it is?'

'As long as that bird doesn't spread its wings and fly,' countered the King, 'all well and good. But once it does, it will smash its way through Heaven itself. As long as it stays silent, that's all there is to it. But once it opens its beak and sings, it will give people one hell of a fright.'

Then the King proceeded to summon seventy-two provincial governors to court. For every one whom he rewarded he punished another. Next he swiftly mustered a great levy and issued forth with his troops. The other states, thrown into a panic, abandoned the territory they had previously captured. For thirty-six years in succession the King maintained his awe-inspiring rule. An account of this is to be found in the Annals of Tian and Wan.

In the eighth year of King Awesome's reign Chu mounted a massive offensive against Qi. The King of Qi sent Baldy to Zhao to ask for relief forces and supplied him with a hundred catties of gold and ten chariots with teams of four, as inducements to Zhao. Baldy Chunyu looked up to the heavens and roared with laughter, so violently that his jaw movement burst his hat-strap.

'Good sir,' said the King, 'am I giving too little?'

'Oh, dear me,' said Baldy, 'I'd never think of suggesting such a thing.'

'Then could you perhaps explain why you are laughing?' asked the King.

'Just now,' said Baldy, 'as I was coming from the eastern part of our country, I saw a man by the roadside performing fertility sacrifices for a good harvest. He was holding just one pig's trotter and one single cup of wine as his offerings, but his prayer went as follows:

BALDY CHUNYU

Grant cartloads from the low ground
and full hampers from the high,
grain in ripe abundance
and sheaves piled to the sky.

When I saw the niggardliness of his offering and the extravagance of his demand, I couldn't help laughing at him.'

King Awesome increased the gifts to twenty-four thousand taels, ten pairs of jade orbs, and a hundred four-horse chariots. Baldy took his leave and set off. On his arrival in Zhao, the King of Zhao gave him a hundred thousand crack troops and a thousand war-chariots. When Chu got word of this, the same night it withdrew its troops.

King Awesome was delighted. He arranged for a special wine-party in his private apartments and invited Baldy to drink with him.

'Good sir,' asked the King, 'how much do you have to shift before you get drunk?'

'Sometimes a gallon, sometimes ten,' replied Baldy.

'If you get drunk on a gallon, good sir,' said the King, 'how come you can ever manage to down ten gallons? I'd be fascinated to know how you explain that one.'

'Your Majesty,' replied Chunyu, 'when I am invited for drinks in your royal presence, with the Minister of Justice at my elbow and the Chief Censor breathing down my neck, I get so nervous bowing and scraping every time I lift my cup, that I'm completely drunk before I've put away a gallon. If I myself am giving a do and entertaining important guests, I fuss around, bowing and bobbing, helping them to drinks, and jumping up and down toasting them with the dregs I've been left. Then it takes me something less than two gallons to get drunk. If I meet old, old friends and companions whom I haven't seen for a long while, we merrily recall old times and talk about things meant only for private consumption. On that sort of occasion it takes five or six gallons to get me drunk. Sometimes, there again, I find myself at a village get-together, all people from the same locality, girls and men sitting close together, and round after round of wine being downed. Games of backgammon and cottabus. . . . Cuddling up in teams and no one giving a damn whose hand you hold. . . . You can give the glad-eye to anyone who takes your fancy. Some of the girls lose their hair-pins, some lose their ear-rings, and . . . Well, I must admit I really get a kick out of dos like that, and I can drink eight gallons and still be only half pissed.

'Or there again, there's the occasion when it goes on really late and you have a really heavy bout of drinking. Find yourselves often all crowded together, with the girls on the men's laps. Slippers and sandals lying around on the floor, cups and plates scattered all over the place. The candles have gone out in the depths of the hall, and the host sees off the other guests and keeps me back. The girls' gossamer silk slips open up and I get a delicate whiff of their bodies' scent. . . . Then I'm really on top of the world and I can put away up to ten gallons. But, yes, that's where the old proverb comes in: *When you go too far with wine, you lose control; a surfeit of pleasure brings a host of sorrows.* It's the same with everything, mind you. You can't go too far with what you say, either. If you do, it spells ruination. That's why some people couch good advice in humour.'

'Very well put,' said the King of Qi, and gave up his all-night boozing parties. He made Baldy Chunyu his chamberlain in charge of receptions for visiting foreign princes and ambassadors, and whenever he attended parties given by the royal clansmen and nobility, Baldy was always at his side.

Jester Meng

JESTER MENG in the Kingdom of Chu was originally a musician. He was six feet tall with a fund of witty repartee at his disposal and was always offering his ruler useful advice in the guise of a good joke.

JESTER MENG

King Solemn of Chu [613 – 591] owned a horse which he loved very much. He clad it in patterned and embroidered garments, installed it in a gorgeous chamber, bedded it down on an open-work carved bed, and fed it with the luxury of dried dates. Eventually the horse became too fat and died. The King had all his ministers mourn for it and wanted to place it in a double-layered coffin and bury it with the rites customarily granted to a grand dignitary. When his entourage argued against such a burial, considering it improper, he issued a decree.

'Anyone who dares to offer me advice about my horse,' he said, 'will be committing a crime punishable by death.'

When this came to the ears of Jester Meng, he entered the throne room looking up to Heaven and weeping loudly. In great consternation the King asked him why he was in such a state.

'It's that horse of yours, Your Majesty,' said Meng. 'You loved him so much. With a great powerful nation like Chu at your disposal anything you want is yours for the asking. Yet all you're giving him is a minister's burial. That's a bit shabby. I beg you to bury him with the rites customarily accorded to a monarch.'

'What's the procedure for that, then?' asked the King.

'I would humbly suggest,' said Jester Meng, 'that you give him an outer coffin of carved jade and an inner coffin of figured catalpa-wood, with end-boards of cedar, maple, pillow-wood, and camphor. Mobilise mailed knights to dig his grave-pit, and let the aged and infants hump the earth. Have the ambassadors of Qi and Zhao form the front escort of the coffin and those of Hân and Wei guard its rear on each flank. Give offerings of royal food for him in your ancestral temple, and perform the Great Sacrifice of Livestock in his honour. Bestow a fief of ten thousand households upon his progeny. In this way, when the rulers of the other states of the world hear the news, they will all know that Your Majesty prizes horses above mere men!'

'How can I have gone so hopelessly wrong?' exclaimed the King. 'What on earth can I do to remedy matters?'

'I suggest,' said the jester, 'that he be buried as one of Your Majesty's royal domestic animals. Let a clay oven serve as his outer coffin, and a bronze tripod cauldron as his inner coffin. Shower him reverently with ginger and dates, strew offerings of magnolia upon him, and sacrifice the purest white rice around him. Enshroud him with the light of fire, and lay him to rest in the bellies of men.'

The King promptly had the horse consigned to his grand chef to avoid a protracted world-wide scandal.

The Chancellor of Chu, Sun Shuao, recognised in Jester Meng an extremely fine character and treated him with great favour. When the Chancellor fell ill, he gave his son some last advice.

'When I'm gone,' said he, 'you're bound to find yourself without a penny to your name. Go then and look up Jester Meng, and tell him you're the son of Sun Shuao.'

Several years passed after his death, and, having indeed found himself in straitened circumstances, the son was reduced to humping firewood for a living. One day he bumped into Jester Meng.

'I'm the son of Sun Shuao,' he told him, 'and on his deathbed my father told me that, should I meet with hard times, I was to go and see you, Jester Meng.'

'Just you stick around, then' said Jester Meng.

Then he dressed himself up in a hat and robes such as those worn by Sun Shuao and set about learning to imitate the former Chancellor's gestures and manner of speech. Within a year or so his imitation was so successful that he was the spitting image of Sun, and even the King of Chu's close attendants were unable to tell the difference.

One day King Solemn held a wine-party. When Jester Meng in disguise stepped forward to toast him and wish him long life, the King was so flabbergasted that he took him to be a reincarnation of Sun Shuao and wanted to appoint him as his Chancellor.

'Well,' Jester Meng demurred, 'allow me to return home to discuss it with my wife before I take up the post.'

To this the King agreed, and three days later Jester Meng was back at court.

'What was your good lady's view on the matter?' asked the King.

'My wife,' replied Meng, 'advised me, whatever I did, never to become Chancellor of Chu. Just not worth it. Take Sun Shuao, for instance. When he was Chancellor he never descended to corruption or underhand fiddles, and he put the whole country in tip-top shape by his first-class government. It was due to him that the King of Chu was able to lord it over all the rulers of the world. But now that he's dead, his son isn't left with enough land to stand a needle on its head in. He's so down and out that he has to lug firewood to keep himself in food and drink. Better to do away with yourself than end up like Sun Shuao. That's what she said. Then she sang a little song:

> '*Sure, it is a hard life,*
> *and the living's rough and rude*
> *in your hovel in the mountains,*
> *ploughing for your food.*
> *And if you get yourself a government post*
> *by methods however vile,*
> *and are meaner and greedier than most,*
> *you can loot yourself a tidy pile,*
> *caring not for fame or face,*
> *indifferent to all disgrace,*
> *living, dying, with no sniff for moral health*
> *you can leave with your kith and kin just rolling*
>   *in the wealth.*

> '*All very nice and jolly,*
> *but I fear there's something more:*
> *if you pocket filthy bribes*
> *and bend the honest law,*
> *with the flood of all your crimes unabated*
> *when you die, your kith and kin*
> *may all be liquidated.*

*'So for all the loot and lucre
one can stack by being sinister,
what's the good of ever being
a greedy-gutted minister?*

*'And yet, and yet, on the other hand,
if you should make a moral stand
and respecting the laws of lord and land
aspire to be a just official
incorrupt and loyal all day long,
tenacious ever of integrity to the very last,
guiltless of all greed or wrong –
why, who's the mug would fall for that?
Just tell me, if you can,
what minister is daft enough
to be an honest man?
For Sun Shuao, the Premier,
was a righteous man all his livelong days:
now his wife and son hawk firewood –
who says that virtue pays?'*

At this, King Solemn allowed Jester Meng to retire and then sent for Sun Shuao's son, upon whom he bestowed Sleeping Hill, a fief of four hundred households, to provide for ancestral sacrifices to Sun Shuao, which have in fact been maintained uninterrupted for ten generations ever since. This sort of information gives one an insight into those times.

Jester Twisty Pole

JESTER TWISTY POLE was an entertainer in Qin, a dwarf and a first-class funster, but behind his every joke was a grasp of universal principles.

JESTER TWISTY POLE

Once the First Emperor of Qin gave a wine-feast during which it poured with rain. The guards on the steps outside the palace were all soaked, and shivered in the cold. Jester Twisty Pole's heart went out to them in their misery.

'Would you chaps care for a spell off duty?' he asked.

'Not half!' they shouted back in chorus.

'As soon as I call you,' he said, 'you must quickly reply with a shout of "Present and reporting for duty, sir!".'

A little while later the official toasts were being given to the Emperor on a daïs at the end of the throne-room and the courtiers were shouting their 'Ten Thousand Years of Long Life!' Jester Twisty Pole leant over the balustrade overlooking the steps and yelled, 'Gentlemen of the guard!'

'Present and reporting for duty, sir!' responded the guards.

'Huh, look at you,' he said, 'great tall, lanky fellows! And what good does it do you? There you are, left out in the rain. While I'm just a short-arsed runt, and here I am taking it easy indoors with the Emperor.'

Hearing this, the Emperor arranged for guard duty to be taken in shifts.

Once, the First Emperor made it known that he intended to set up a great game-reserve extending all the way from Box Valley Pass in the east to Granary Store in Yong to the west.

'What a marvellous idea!' said Jester Twisty Pole. 'You could let loose a whole mass of wild beasts and birds in it. And then, if there's an invasion, you can just let the gazelles and deer butt the invaders with their horns. That'll send them packing!'

That was enough to make the First Emperor drop his scheme.

When the Second Emperor [209 – 207] ascended the throne, he wanted to lacquer the Great Wall.

'That's a splendid idea,' said Jester Twisty Pole. 'If you hadn't mentioned it, Your Majesty, I would certainly have suggested it myself. It might mean an awful lot of toil and trouble for the ordinary people, but all the same it's a magnificent project. Lacquer the Great Wall all smooth and shiny, then it will be too slippery for any invaders to climb over it. Now, let's get down to the practical side of the job. The lacquering is easy enough, but building a drying room may present a problem or two.'

The Second Emperor burst out laughing and shelved his project.

Not long afterwards the Second Emperor was slain and Jester Twisty Pole went over to the Han forces and enjoyed a few more years under the new dynasty.

Historical Commentary

Here follows the Grand Historian's commentary:

> *Old Baldy Chunyu laughed like hell,*
> *the King of Qi ran riot beyond belief,*
> *Jester Meng shook his head in song*
> *and the firewood carrier picked up a fief.*
> *One shout from Jester Twisty Pole*
> *and wretched guards gained sweet relief.*
>
> WERE THESE NOT ALL GREAT MEN, TOO?

* *
*